Edward A. (Edward Adderley) Stopford

The Talk Of The Road

Edward A. (Edward Adderley) Stopford

The Talk Of The Road

ISBN/EAN: 9783742840929

Manufactured in Europe, USA, Canada, Australia, Japa

Cover: Foto ©Andreas Hilbeck / pixelio.de

Manufactured and distributed by brebook publishing software
(www.brebook.com)

Edward A. (Edward Adderley) Stopford

The Talk Of The Road

PREFACE.

————◆————

If the reader should recognise something of the dry humour and originality of the Irish peasantry in what follows, the writer feels that it is not attributable to any powers of invention, imagination, or wit which he himself can lay claim to, but simply to the circumstance of his having spent his life among the Irish people, and been an attentive observer of their habits and modes of thought. Those who have, like the writer, lived in Ireland, will recognise the peculiarities of the Irish mind; for it is, in truth, many a poor Irishman, whom the writer has personally known or heard of, that is speaking in these pages. There is scarcely an incident related which has not actually occurred, many of them within his personal knowledge, and most of the others under the immediate observation of his friends. A few, which have been objected to as the most improbable, are, in fact, those which he has the greatest assurance are actual facts.

For the originality which may sometimes appear in the mode of expression, the writer can claim but little credit, for he has but recorded faithfully the expressions which plain men have actually used in their own plain way; and he begs the reader to remember that the influence of a peculiar language on modes of thought sometimes survives the general use of the language itself; and when Irishmen come to speak English they, almost of necessity, use it in an Irish fashion.

Whatever may be the issue of the struggle going on between the rival Churches, all well-disposed persons feel that it should be conducted with moderation, and without physical violence or abuse. That there are many individuals among the Roman Catholic priesthood who would not condescend to the vulgar expedients occasionally alluded to in what follows, must be admitted even by their opponents ; but that, on the other hand, there are not a few Father Johns in Ireland, who *prefer* abuse and violence to calm reasoning, no person acquainted with country life in Ireland will deny. That the exertions of all good men who wish well to their country, to soften the tone and moderate the acerbity of party feeling, and encourage the progress of truth by calm reasoning, may be successful, is the most ardent wish of the writer.

E. A. S.

CONTENTS.

TALK OF THE ROAD.

CHAPTER I.

WHAT SETS PEOPLE ASTRAY.

ONE Sunday, after chapel, Pat Dolan and Jemmy Brannan were going home from Mass; and as Pat, who was before, stopped to speak to a neighbour, Jem overtook him, and they walked on together.

"Good morrow, Jem," says Pat.

"Good morrow kindly, Pat."

And so they fell to talking of the sermon, for Father John had preached that day.

"Didn't Father John give it to the Bible readers like himself to-day?" said Pat.

"'Deed and he did, and it's he that can," said Jem.

"I wonder how Tim Finnegan and Peter Daly, that I know is reading the Bible, liked to hear him; maybe that will stop them, or maybe they will go on till Father John puts up their names before the people," said Pat.

"I don't know," said Jem, "but I see that

them that takes to reading is not easily put from it.   But Father John said óne thing to-day that bothers me entirely ; I can't see the reason of it at all."

" Now, what was that ? " said Pat.

" Why, he told us," said Jem, " that any man that takes to reading the Bible will be sure to turn Protestant : and I can't come up to the raison of that at all."

" Why, man alive," said Pat, " don't you see it yourself ? Isn't there Tim Daly and Mat Fogarty, and plenty more, and Johnny Connor himself, that was sexton of the chapel, that Father John trusted more than any man in the parish ; and didn't they all turn Protestants when they took to reading the Bible ? and what for should you be saying that you can't understand Father John saying that, when you see it yourself as plain as the blessed sun in the sky at this moment ? "

" True for you, Pat," said Jemmy ; " I see all that as plain as you do, and maybe a little more ; for I see foreby that it is mostly the best Catholic, and the most devotest man, and the man that minds his duty best, and the greatest arguer against the Protestants, that evermore turns

Protestant, all out and out—the surest of all, once he takes to reading the Bible in earnest; none of your keeping it quiet in the bottom of the chest with the likes of them; but they'll turn Readers too, and go through fire and water to get others to read and turn Protestant, like themselves. I see that; and I don't wonder that Father John *says it;* for sure he would be blind all out not to see what every man in the parish sees. So it isn't Father John *saying it* that bothers me; but what I can't make out at all is, *why* the Bible should put every one astray, and make every one that reads it turn Protestant."

"Man alive," said Pat, "sure isn't that as plain as your hand? Why, wasn't Luther the first Protestant that ever lived, and didn't he write all the Bible himself, and why wouldn't it turn every one Protestant that reads it?"

"Sure enough, Pat," said Jem, "if that was true it would make all plain; but there isn't a word of truth in it, that's all. Sure, doesn't Father John tell us that the Catholic religion is 1850 years old, and doesn't he tell us that Luther lived only 300 years ago (and I believe that's all true)? and will any man in his senses tell me that the

Catholic Church had never a Bible for 1,550 years ? Sure that doesn't stand to reason. And isn't there the Douay Bible, that the priest allows is the true one ? And where did that come from ? Sure Luther didn't write that too. And so, if Father John was to tell us that Luther wrote all the Bible out of his own head (and, sure enough, I heard Father John once say very near that same) I wouldn't believe him ; for how could Luther put it on the priests, too ? "

"Don't you see, Jem," said Pat, "that you have it now ? 'Twas the Protestant Bible, of course, that Luther wrote ; and it's as different from the Catholic Bible as turnips is from the good ould Cups (my blessing be with them and the ould times), and sure that's the reason that reading the Protestant Bible turns every one into a Protestant."

"Well, Pat," said Jem, " if that was it I'd be quite happy and settled in my mind at once ; but I doubt it isn't, after all. Didn't I hear old John Dowd, the schoolmaster that lives over at Kilmore, the cutest and learnedst man that ever was in this country, say that he got a Protestant Bible and a Catholic Bible, and that he read them both together (and he was the boy that was fit to read two books at wonst), and didn't I hear him lay it down that there wasn't a word of differ between them that signified one haporth ?   And that's what makes me ever more uneasy in my mind, till I get the reason why reading the Bible should make people turn Protestant. Sure now it's not easy to believe that the Word of God would put every one astray entirely. And, by the same token, you told me yourself that Luther was the first Protestant that ever lived, only 300 years ago, and that there never was a Protestant for 1,500 years before that. Now, if they had the Bible all those 1,500 years, isn't it mighty odd if no one ever looked into it ? and if they did, why did it never turn them Protestants before as well as after ?"

"Maybe it was all in Latin, Jem," said Pat, "and that nobody at all could read it."

"Well," said Jem, "the schoolmaster said that wasn't it, though I don't remember how he made it out. But I'll tell you what it is, Pat : my mind's all astray about thinking why the Bible should make every one a Protestant, and set every one astray that reads it. Sure that isn't like the Word of God at all : and I can't attend to my duties the way I used to do, nor keep myself from thinking, and I be to look for something to quiet me, and it's to Father John I'll go, and ask him the reason why reading the Word of God is setting all the people astray."

" And isn't it yourself that 'ill have to flatter him neatly, and get him in the best of good humour, when you go to poke him with questions like that, Jem ? " said Pat. " And isn't it his reverence that'll handle you, and maybe put up your name before the people ? "

"Well, Pat," said Jem, "I want to be satisfied in my mind, and sure I'm willing to be satisfied ; and who would I go to to settle me if I wouldn't go to my own clergy ? Sure, if all the boys that go astray from reading would only go to their clergy to satisfy them, and set them right, maybe it wouldn't be so bad. Any way I'm resolved to try ; and maybe I'll have the telling you what he says."

And by that time Jem was got to his own door ; so he said, " Good evening, Pat."

" Good evening, neighbour," said Pat, " and I wish you safe from Father John."

Well, it so happened, about three weeks after, that Pat and Jemmy fell in together again, coming home from chapel, and of course they began to talk.

"And did you ever speak to Father John?" said Pat.

"Indeed I did," said Jem; "last Thursday was a fortnight he overtook me on the road, him riding and I walking; so I took off my hat to his reverence, and, as he spoke to me pretty civil, I made bold to talk to him then; and says I, 'Your reverence, I hope since you came to this parish you never found me anything but a boy that always attended to his duties and was respectful to his clergy.' 'True for you,' says he, 'that's what you are.' 'Well, then,' says I, 'I want a bit of advice, and maybe a little instruction from your reverence; for who would I go to for it only to my own clergy?' 'Quite right,' says he; 'if everybody did that,' says he, 'the way they used to do, the people wouldn't be going astray.' 'Well, then, your reverence,' says I, 'I'm unasy in my mind about one thing that's disturbing me; and I'm sure your reverence could settle it in one word, and maybe you'll have the kindness to do so.' 'What is it?' says he, quite pleasant-like. 'I wanted to know, your reverence,' says I, 'what is the reason that the Word of God should set everybody astray that reads it?' With that he turned round upon me, as sudden as a clap of thunder, and says he, 'It's reading the Bible you are, and going to turn Protestant on me.' 'No, please your reverence,' says I, 'it's nothing of the kind.' 'You're a liar,' says he, 'and it's reading the Bible you are.' 'No, please your reverence,' says I, 'I never had a Bible in my hand in all my life, and I never heard one word read out of it good or bad' (and with that he began to look more easy in his mind and more agreeable-like), 'barring,' says I, 'the bits of scraps that your reverence reads in the chapel sometimes, and sure,' says I, looking up at him out of the corner of my eye, 'that wasn't too much, any way.' 'And what more do you want ?' says he. 'Only just to know,' says I, 'why it is that the reading of God's Word puts every one astray that reads it.' 'And what's that to you,' says he, 'if *you* don't read it ?' 'Only this, your reverence,' says I, 'that I see everybody that's reading the Bible going astray and turning Protestant.' 'Sure enough,' says he. 'And it seems so unnatural like,' says I, 'that God's own Word should set the people astray, and ruin them entirely, that I can't get my mind off thinking of it, and I can't attend to my duties for thinking ; and sure if your reverence could settle my mind for me in one word, wouldn't it be the good thing for me ?' 'To be sure,' says he, 'and isn't that what I am going to do in a moment ?' and with that I pulls off my hat, and says he, 'Isn't it the Protestant Bible they're reading,' says he, 'that's all full of lies from beginning to end ? and isn't that the reason they're going astray and turning heretics, and doesn't it stand to reason ?' says he. 'Oh, then, your reverence,' says I, 'it's all because they're reading a false Bible that they are going astray and turning heretics.' 'To be sure it is,' says he ; 'what else ?' 'And if the Catholic Bible wouldn't set them astray,' says I, 'I'm all right in my mind, and satisfied entirely now and ever-more.' 'To be sure it wouldn't,' says he, 'when it's the right one.' 'Well, your reverence,' says I, 'just one word more. When so many of the people is turning, and,' says I, 'there's Johnny Connor and Tim Daly, and there's——.' 'Don't talk to me about them,' says he ; 'I don't want to hear of the likes of them.' 'Well, it isn't about them, your reverence,' says I, 'but about the rest of the boys that isn't gone yet. If it's a bad Bible that's leading them astray, wouldn't it be the good thing just to give them the right one, and let them see the differ ?' 'What's that to you ?'

CHAPTER II.

THE TWO BIBLES.

WELL, a few days after Jemmy Brannan made
up his mind to speak to the Rev. Mr. Owens, it
happened that Jemmy and Pat Dolan were working together for a farmer ; and they were filling
a cart out of some manure-heaps that lay on the
roadside. And, as they were working, who should
come up the road but Mr. Owens himself. Now,
Mr. Owens seldom passed people by without
saying a word ; for he was a pleasant-spoken
man, and Irishmen like a gentleman that speaks
free and pleasant. So Mr. Owens said, "It's a
fine day for the work, boys ; thanks be to God
for it."

"A fine day, your reverence, God be praised,"
said Jem, very well pleased to have Mr. Owens
to speak to that day.

"It would be bad farming without the dung,
boys," said Mr. Owens.

"Sure enough, your reverence, that would be
bad work," said Pat ; "but there's a deal of poor
creatures has little dung to put on it since the
praties went."

"And without the spade or the plough the dung is not much good," said the parson.

"I'm thinking both spade and plough will have to go deeper these times," said Jem.

"Did you ever hear of Jesus Christ digging and dunging?" said Mr. Owens.

"No, your reverence," said both the men, dropping their spades in great amazement.

"Why, did you never read of that in the Bible?" said Mr. Owens.

"No, your reverence," said Jem, "I never did."

"What Bible is it in, your reverence?" said Pat; "is it in the Protestant Bible or the Catholic Bible?"

"And which of these do you read?" said Mr. Owens. Pat did not like to say he never read a word of either in his life, so he said nothing, and Mr. Owens went on—"I believe it is just the same in both, as I could show you if I had the books."

"Well, your reverence," said Jem, "that is just what I would like to see."

"What?" said Mr. Owens.

"The differ between the two books," said Jem.

"Well, if that is all you want to see," said Mr.

"APPROBATION.

"This new edition of the English version of the Bible, printed, with our permission, by Richard Coyne, 4, Capel-street, carefully collated, by our direction, with the Clementine Vulgate ; likewise, with the Douay version of the Old Testament of 1509,* and with the Rhemish version of the New Testament of 1582, and with other approved English versions—WE, by our authority, approve. And WE declare that the same may be used, with great spiritual profit, by the faithful; provided it be read with due reverence, and the proper dispositions.—Given at Dublin, 2nd September, 1829."

And then Mr. Owens showed them that this approbation was signed by "Daniel Murray, D.D.," the late Roman Catholic Archbishop of Dublin ; and he showed them this added to it—"We concur with the above approbation," signed by twenty-four of the Irish Roman Catholic bishops. So Jem and Pat were both satisfied that this was the right book, and Pat was more easy in his mind ; for after reading this he thought it could be no harm for him to look into it ; and so

* This date, 1509, must be a misprint, for the Douay version of the Old Testament was published for the *first time* in the year 1609.

he kept this book in his hand, and Mr. Owens handed the other to Jem.

"Now, where would you like to read?" said Mr. Owens.

"Oh, your reverence can choose better than we can," said Jem.

So Mr. Owens opened the Church of England Bible at the First Epistle of Timothy, chap. ii., verse 5, and Jem read as follows—"For there is one God, and one Mediator between God and men, the man Christ Jesus."

"Holy Kitty!" exclaimed Jem.

"Stop a minute, my friend," said the parson, laying his hand on Jem's arm; "who was Kitty?"

"Why, then, indeed, your reverence," said Jem, "I don't know, barrin' she might be one of the saints."

"And you will swear by you don't know who? Do you know what our Saviour says about swearing?" said the parson.

"I suppose 'Thou shalt not take the name of God in vain,'" said Jem; "but what harm is it to swear by Holy Kitty?"

"Is it not harm to do what Christ commands us not to do?" said Mr. Owens.

"Surely," said Jem, "there's no denying that."

"Well," said Mr. Owens, "listen to the words of Christ himself, in his own Sermon on the Mount (Matthew v. 34), '*I say to you not to swear at all*,' and in v. 37, '*Let your speech be yea, yea ; no, no : and that which is over and above these is of evil.*' And the Apostle St. James, in his epistle, says (chapter v. 12), 'But, above all things, my brethren, swear not; neither by heaven, nor by the earth, nor by any other oath ; but let your speech be yea, yea ; no, no ; that you fall not under judgment.' Now, I ask you, my friends," said the parson, "can it be safe for us to swear by *any* oath, when we have such directions from God about our talk ?"

"Surely not, your reverence," said Jem.

"And if God has given us such directions, ought we not to keep them ? and can we keep them without knowing them ? Now, did you ever know this before, that Christ had given us orders not to swear by any oath ?"

"I never heard it before," said Jem.

"You see, then," said Mr. Owens, "what need we have to study God's Word, in order that we may know what God commands us to do or not to do. If we do not know his Word, we may be continually doing the very things that make him angry. But come back to the verse you read, Jem; it seemed to strike you forcibly."

"Holy Virgin!" exclaimed Jem.

"Stop again, my friend," said the parson; "are you not doing again the very thing that your Saviour bid you not do?"

"I am, your reverence," said Jem; "but it's so hard for a man to quit, in a moment, what he was used to all his life."

"You see, then," said the parson, "what need we have to study Christ's words, and to learn them carefully, that we may keep them. That is the reason that we teach the Bible to our children, that they may learn to avoid habits that are so displeasing to God, and so hard to get rid of. The Jews were told to teach them to their children; and why not to Christian children? And St. Paul praised Timothy for knowing them from a child. And you see now what need there is that the Church should teach Christ's words carefully to people; for it is not once hearing them that will do; we must read and study them again and again, to learn to keep them. And this is why we teach the Bible so much."

"But, your reverence," said Pat, "I hear Protestants swear betimes; and how comes that, if they get such instruction?"

"And many," said Mr. Owens, "that heard our Saviour teach, and his Apostles too, were never the better, but the worse of what they heard. Very likely that some that heard that Sermon on the Mount went on swearing; but that was no fault of the teaching. The Church ought to teach Christ's words, whether men will hear them and do them or not. But come back to our verse; what were you going to say of it, Jem?"

"I was going to say, your reverence," said Jem (and he didn't swear this time), "if them isn't the very words that made Johnny Connor, the sexton to the chapel, turn Protestant. Sure I heard him myself, when Father John taxed him in the chapel, forenent the people, with reading, and wanted to take his Bible, and Johnny wouldn't give it. 'And what do you find in it,' says Father John, 'that you won't give it up?' 'I find in it,' says Johnny, 'that there is one Mediator between God and men.' I mind the words well. Now, Pat," said Jem, turning sharp round on Pat as he spoke, "look at your book, man, and see if the words is there; and then we will see which book set Johnny Connor astray."

" Read it again in your own book first," said the parson, "and then we will see the 'differ' exactly."

So Jem read again, *For there is one God, and one Mediator between God and men, the man Christ Jesus.*"

" Now, my friend, will you read?" said the parson to Pat. So Pat read, "*For there is one God and one Mediator of God and men, the man Christ Jesus.*"

" Now," said the parson, "which Bible set Johnny Connor astray?"

" Well, that's plain, anyway," said Jem; "there's but one Mediator; and the one book is as good as the other for that."

" What would you like to have next?" said Mr. Owens. So both told him to choose, for they were at a loss.

" Can you say the commandments?" said Mr. Owens.

" Yes, your reverence," said both of them.

So Mr. Owens turned to Jem, "Say the first commandment;" so Jem said, "Thou shalt have no other gods but me." Then Mr. Owens turned to Pat, and said, "Say the second commandment."

So Pat repeated, "Thou shalt not take the name of God in vain."

"Is there nothing else between the two?" said Mr. Owens.

"No, your reverence," said both Pat and Jem together.

"Were you never taught that something was left out?" said Mr. Owens.

"No, your reverence," said they both. So Mr. Owens opened the two Bibles, and made them read what was left out in their catechisms; and Jem read first out of the Protestant book—"Thou shalt not make unto thee any graven image, or any likeness of anything that is in heaven above, or that is in the earth beneath, or that is in the water under the earth: Thou shalt not bow down thyself to them, nor serve them; for I the Lord thy God am a jealous God, visiting the iniquity of the fathers upon the children unto the third and fourth generation of them that hate me, and showing mercy unto thousands of them that love me, and keep my commandments." And then Pat read out of the Roman Catholic Bible—"Thou shalt not make to thyself a graven thing, nor the likeness of anything that is in heaven above, or in the earth beneath, nor of those things that are in the waters under the earth.   Thou shalt not adore them, nor serve them : I am the Lord thy God, mighty, jealous, visiting the iniquity of the fathers upon the children, unto the third and fourth generation of them that hate me ; and showing mercy unto thousands to them that love me, and keep my commandments."—Exodus xx. 4, 5, 6 (Douay Bible).

"I don't see 'images' in the Catholic Bible, your reverence," said Pat.

"And what *can* a graven thing mean but a graven image ?" said Mr. Owens.

"Never mind that, your reverence," said Jem. "I see the word '*likeness*' in *both books* ; and if we must not make a '*likeness*' of anything in heaven, how can we make an image of it ?"

"Now, then," said Mr. Owens, "you see what God said in his commandments, and you never knew that before."

"Well, that beats all, your reverence," said Jem ; "the two Bibles is like enough ; and the Catholic Bible that we *don't* see, and the Catholic catechism that we *do* see and learn, is not like at all."

"And that, too," said Mr. Owens, "in the matter of God's own commandments, that he spoke himself. And how shall we know how to serve God if we do not know his own commandments?" And here Mr. Owens showed them, in the Douay Bible, the words just before the ten commandments of God—" 'And the Lord spoke ALL THESE WORDS.' Now, if God spoke all these words in giving his commandments, should not we *learn* THEM ALL, when we learn the commandments? And here, you see, we should not put our trust in any church or man to teach us God's commandments, but we should look in the Bible, to see what God commanded. But it's getting late," said Mr. Owens ; "maybe you would come in some other night ?"

"Indeed, an' we will," said Jem ; "but I'd like to have the book at home."

"Which book ?" said Mr. Owens. So then Pat and Jem began debating ; for Pat wanted the Catholic book, for he was still afraid the Protestant book might set him astray ; so at last they agreed that Jem should take the Protestant Bible, and Pat the Douay Bible, and read them together, verse about, in the evenings, till they found all the " differ ;" and so Jem asked the price of his book. "A shilling," said the parson; so Jem paid it, well pleased. And then, Pat pulled out his shilling.

"Oh," said Mr. Owens, "this book is four and sixpence."

"Four and sixpence, your reverence!" said Pat; "and sure Jem's is the purtiest book; for it has a real leather cover on it, and this is only paper; and Jem's is only a shilling."

"I can't help that," said Mr. Owens; "we can't get this book for less."*

"I see now, your reverence," said Jem, "it's the Protestants that want the poor to have the Bible any way, when they make it cheap." And so the parson agreed to give Pat his book for two and sixpence, and to take it at sixpence a week: and when they were going out, Mr. Owens said—"I hope, boys, you don't think that I set you astray."

"And does your reverence not want us to leave the Catholic Church?" said Pat.

"If St. Peter or St. Paul was to preach tomorrow," said Mr. Owens, "would you listen to

---

* We are glad to hear that the Douay Bible may now be procured at 2s. 6d., published by Simms and M'Intyre, Belfast. —ED.

them ? or if they wrote you a letter would you read it ?"

" Surely, your reverence," said Pat, "I would."

"And would that make you leave the Catholic Church ? " said Mr. Owens.

" It couldn't, your reverence," said Pat.

" Well," said Mr. Owens, " I give you the letters they wrote to you, and to all.   If I saw St. Peter or St. Paul I would not ask them to leave the Catholic Church ; and no more would I ask you : I want you to be such Catholics as St. Peter and St. Paul were—no more, and no less ; and for that I give you their writings to read.   Judge for yourselves, my friends, for you have common sense, like most Irishmen, whether they who give you St. Peter and St. Paul's writings, or they who keep them from you, are most in earnest in wanting you to be such Catholics as St. Paul and St. Peter were."

So they left Mr. Owens for that night ; and if we hear of anything more, it won't be lost.

CHAPTER III.

THE GLORIES OF MARY.

WE have not lost sight of Pat and Jem yet, and perhaps our readers may like to know what we have heard. Well, a few days ago, they were setting potatoes for a farmer, working one at each side of the same ridge; and their dinner was brought to them in a tin can and a wooden plate tied up in a cloth, and they sat down under a thorn bush to eat it; and, when they had done, Pat pulled a book out of his pocket, and Jem leaned over his shoulder, reading with him, till the bell would ring for work. And while they were reading, Father John rode down the lane; and though they did not see him, for their backs were towards him, he saw they were over a book.

Now, Father John was getting mighty uneasy in his mind when he saw people reading; so he gave his horse to a boy in the lane, and he walked up quiet, till he got just at their backs, and, "What book is that you're reading, boys?" says he.

"Please your reverence," said Pat, holding up

the book, "it's 'The Glories of Mary,'" and very glad Pat was that time that it wasn't his Douay Bible he had in his hand.

"Oh, that's all right," said Father John; "that's a good book; where did you get it?"

"Please your reverence," said Pat, "I bought it from Judy Brannigan, down at John Dolan's wake."

"Ah, Judy is a useful woman among the people," said Father John: "she is always selling good books among them."

"And, indeed, your reverence," said Jem, "she made great brags of all she sold of this book; she says there is more of it in the parish now than all other books put together."

"So much the better," said his reverence; "there can't be too much of that book; that's a real Catholic book, and I am glad to see you reading it, boys."

And with that Father John was going away, well satisfied in his mind; when Jem stopped him by saying,

"And is it true, your reverence, that the man who wrote it was made a saint by the Pope, just thirteen years ago, in the year 1839?"

"Quite true," says Father John.

" An'd was that the year he died, your reverence ? " said Pat.

" Oh, no," said Father John, " he died more than 150 years before that."

" And why didn't they make him a saint before ? " said Pat.

" Oh, it takes a long time," said Father John, " the Church is so particular."

" And didn't the cardinals at Rome read this book, and certify that there was nothing in it against faith or morals ?"* said Jem.

" To be sure they did," said Father John ; " he couldn't be made a saint without that."

" Well, it ought to be the good book," said Jem.

" Of course it must, when it was written by a saint of the Holy Catholic Church," said Father John ; " and I am glad to see that it's such books you are reading, boys."

And with that Father John was going away ; but Jem stopped him with a question.

" Maybe your reverence would explain one thing in the book to me," said Jem.

* It would seem that Jem must have got a copy of an edition published some years ago, in the preface of which all this was related. Everything about Alphonso Liguori being made a saint is left out of the later editions ; we wonder why.—ED.

Now, Father John was so well pleased to see Jem at this book, instead of the Bible, that he stopped to answer him. "And what is it?" said he.

"Well, your reverence," said Jem, "is Mary the mediator between God and man?"

"No," said Father John, "Jesus Christ is the mediator between God and man; but then Mary is our mediator with Jesus Christ."

"Well, your reverence," said Jem, "I find that in this book, sure enough;" and Father John seemed pleased at that; "but I find more in the book foreby," said Jem; and he looked to the page that he and Pat were at, and he read (page 257)—"I am, says Mary, the defence of all who have recourse to me, and my mercy is to them a tower of refuge, and therefore have I been appointed by my Lord the MEDIATRIX of peace BETWEEN SINNERS AND GOD." And then Jem turned back to page 252, and read, "O Mary, thy office is TO MEDIATE BETWEEN GOD AND MEN." "Is that right, your reverence?" said Jem.

"And why wouldn't it be right," said Father John, "when it's in a Catholic book, that the Holy Church approves?"

"Because, your reverence," said Jem, "it's in

the Bible that *there is one mediator between God and men, the man Christ Jesus;* and I don't see how both can be true."

"Didn't I say it was reading the Bible you were?" said Father John.

"And if it wasn't true when your reverence said it, it's true now anyway," said Jem.

"And if you will be reading heretical books," said Father John, "how can I help your going astray?"

"But, your reverence," said Pat, "is not that in the Catholic Bible too?"

"What do you know about that?" said Father John.

"Please your reverence," said Pat, "sure it's the Catholic Bible that I have; and sure, your reverence, that isn't a bad book."

And at that Father John looked less pleased than ever, but he was not just ready with an answer, and Pat did not want to talk much about that; so Pat went on—"But *did* the Blessed Virgin say that she was appointed the mediatrix between sinners and God? or where did she say it?"

"How do I know?" said Father John, getting out of all patience at being so bothered.

"Sure, your reverence, didn't I read it out of

this book ?" said Jem, holding up the " Glories of Mary."

" I'll tell you what," said Father John, turning round upon Jem, " if it's reading the Bible you are, you'll soon be out of the Catholic Church, and out of that there is no salvation.   Didn't I often tell you that the Bible would set you astray ?"

" Well, your reverence, that's not it," said Jem ; "for while I was only reading the Bible I was getting quite contented in my mind, and I was hoping I would go on reading it, and never leave the Catholic Church at all, until I came across this book, and now it's *it* that is setting my mind astray ; for sure when the Bible tells me that there is only one mediator between God and men, and this book, that your reverence says is a Catholic book, says it is Mary's office to mediate between God and men ; sure if I can't get some way of settling between them, it will put me astray entirely."

" I'll tell you the way," said Father John, for he was getting afraid of losing Jem entirely ; doesn't this book itself tell you that Jesus Christ is the *only mediator of justice ?* but that does not hinder Mary to be the mediator of grace and of peace."

" And, please your reverence," said Jem, "does-

not this book say (page 262), that Mary was
'*chosen from eternity to be the Mother of God,
that her mercy might procure salvation for those
whom the justice of her son could not save,*' and
doesn't that make *her* a BETTER mediator of salvation than if she was the mediator of justice
itself? and isn't that worse and worse?"

"I knew how it would be," said Father John,
"when you took to reading the Bible; you're
going straight out of the Catholic Church, and
out of that there's no redemption, and you'll
never have a Mass said for your soul when you're
dead; and what for will you go out of the
Catholic Church?"

"If ever I be driven out of it, your reverence," said Jem, "it will be for one thing
only."

"And what's that?" said Father John.

"To have the Lord Jesus Christ for my
Saviour, and Him only," said Jem.

"And who told you there was any other
Saviour in the Catholic Church?" said Father
John.

"This book, your reverence," said Jem, "the
'Glories of Mary,' that your reverence says was
written by a saint, and approved of by the Pope

and the cardinals; this book that your reverence says can never set me astray. Sure I turned down the page when I came to it, and here it is —'*When we ask of God his graces, he sends us to Mary, saying,* GO TO MARY' (page 220), and where did God say that at all, or who did he say it to?" said Jem; "and here it goes on—'Our salvation is in the hand of Mary;' and, 'He who is protected by Mary is saved; he who is not protected by her is lost' (page 221); and sure here is a prayer to her—'O pure and immaculate Queen, SAVE ME, *deliver me from eternal damnation*' (page 220); and here again—'Her mercy procures salvation for those the justice of her Son could not save' (page 362); and is not all that making her the Saviour?"

"Let alone this book," said Father John; "I'm sorry you ever came across it."

"And sure, your reverence," said Jem, "you know well there is more of this book in the parish than there is of the Bible; and many's the time I heard your reverence preach against reading the Bible, and did you ever say a word against this book? And didn't you tell me just now that this book would never set me astray, or put me from the Catholic Church, and that the Bible would put me astray from the Catholic Church? And isn't that the poor case? to say that the writings of man will keep us in the church, and that the writings of God will put us out of it? Isn't that enough to drive a man to think that it is not the Church of God at all? Isn't it——"

"Stop there, will you?" said Father John; "it's not for me to be standing here, arguing with the like of you."

"And it's not for the like of me to be talking this way with your reverence," said Jem, "only for my soul, that you say will be damned if I read the Word of God; and who will I talk to if I don't to my clergy? And sure if your reverence would only read the Catholic Bible to us, and explain it to us, that we mightn't go astray in it—if your reverence would only do that for us——"

"I'll tell you what I'll do for you," said Father John, for he was getting really angry now: "it's on the altar I'll curse you next Sunday; I'll curse you with bell, book, and candle. No man in the parish shall give you employment, no one shall buy or sell with you, no man shall work with you; and if this man

digs at the other side of the ridge with you, I
will · curse him too ; and see what your Bible
will do for you then."

" Then, your reverence," said Jem, " I'll see if
I can't get a blessing from God under all."

And so Father John went off to his horse (and,
indeed, he was mighty cross to the boy that held
it for him), and the bell rung for work ; so · Pat
and Jem could not talk any more ; but if they
did talk afterwards, we hope to find out all
about it.

The writer thinks it well to say a few words
of the book that Pat and Jem got hold of.

He believes it was first printed in English in
this country soon after the writer, St. A¹phonso
Liguori, with two or three others, were canonized
(or made saints) by the Pope of Rome, in the
year 1839, and the writer believes the first edition
then published in Ireland contained an account
of St. Alphonso having been made a saint by the
Church of Rome, and also a copy of the certificate which the cardinals were required to give on
that occasion, that they had read all St. Alphonso's works, and that there was nothing
found in them CONTRARY TO FAITH or morals.

This certificate was then taken hold of by the Protestants, to fix the doctrines contained in this book upon the Church of Rome; and this, perhaps, is the reason why all mention of St. Alphonso's canonization, and of the certificate of the cardinals, is left out of the editions since published. But the circulation of the book was not stopped; several editions have since been published in Ireland, in a very cheap form, and tens of thousands of copies have been circulated; and the writer cannot find that any priest in Ireland has ever tried to stop it, or has publicly expressed disapprobation of the doctrines contained in it.

The edition which the writer possesses is that of 1845. The title is as follows :—

"The Glories of Mary. First Part. A Paraphrase on the Salve Regina, &c., &c. Translated from the Italian of St. Alphonsus Liguori, *by a Catholic clergyman.* Dublin: Published by James Duffy, 23, Anglesea-street, 1845."

It is from this edition, as being that in most common use, that the writer has marked the pages referred to by Jem.

Some idea may be formed of the book, from

the titles which St. Alphonso has prefixed to his chapters. The following are a few specimens (ch. ii., sec. 1):—"MARY IS OUR LIFE, because *she* obtains for us the pardon of our sins." Where note that the Douay Bible says—"Jesus said to her (Martha), I am the resurrection and THE LIFE."—John xi. 25. And again—"Your LIFE is hid with Christ in God."—Ep. to Colos. iii. 3. And—"When Christ shall appear, WHO IS YOUR LIFE."—v. 4. But not one word in the Douay Bible about Mary being our life.

Again, St. Alphonso gives this heading to chapter 3—(1), "Mary is the hope of all. (2), Mary is the hope of sinners." Whereas the Douay Bible says—"Christ in you the hope of glory."—Ep. to Coloss. i. 27. And again—"Christ Jesus, our hope."—1st Ep. to Timothy i. 1. But not one word in the Douay Bible of Mary being our hope.

Again, St. Alphonso puts this title to chapter 6, section 3—"Mary is the peacemaker of sinners with God." Whereas the Douay Bible says—"We have peace with God, through our Lord Jesus Christ."—Rom. v. 1. And—"HE is our peace."—Eph. ii. 14. But not one word in the Douay Bible about Mary being the peacemaker of sinners with God. This will give a fair idea of this book—"The Glories of Mary" —which all true Catholics, who read the Douay Bible, will acknowledge to be a fearful book for the Church of Rome to make herself answerable for, and allow to be circulated unrestrained among her people.

———

CHAPTER IV.

THE STONE AND THE PRATY.

WELL, Father John did not curse Jem after all ; at least, not this time. Maybe Father John thought it hard to take the bit out of the mouths of Jem's children ; or maybe there were too many to be cursed ; or maybe Father John had read the report of what took place at the Antrim Assizes in March, 1846, and seen what came of the priest cursing the miller.

But Pat and Jem did not know yet that the curse was not going to be now ; and so it happened, the next day, when they sat down to dinner under the thorn bush, they began to talk of it.

"And what made him so angry entirely ?"

said Pat. "Sure we only wanted him to set us right ; and if he would only take the trouble to teach us what is right, sure we would be willing to be taught by him, and give him every respect. And sure if we just went on as we used to do, and never offered to learn anything at all about God, or the Bible, or the Saviour of sinners, we would never get a cross word from him no more than some of the boys that thinks no more about religion than the horses and cows does ; and yet Father John has nothing but a pleasant word for them ; and I never see him get cross entirely till it's the Bible that's in it ; and what's the reason he was so angry ?"

"Indeed," said Jem, "that's what I'm thinking of all day ; and there's something in it that's not right ; for ask him what I will out of the Bible, to get him to explain it to me, or set me right, it's not about that thing he'll speak in his answer at all : just as if he didn't care how far I went astray in it : but it's always the one answer he has, ' It's reading the Bible you are,' says he—that's his cry ; as if the very name of it angered him, so that he could not teach us anything out of it at all."

"And maybe that's just near the truth," said

Pat. "Maybe it's little he knows it himself, and he's afraid to take on him to teach it."

"Well, I'd think that too," said Jem, "*only that he gets so angry about it.* For when I see that look in his face, when he hears of the Bible, it isn't like as if he didn't know it at all himself; it's a deal liker as if he knew it too well, and that it wouldn't be on his side; and sure it's *that* that *would* make him angry in earnest, and nothing else that I can see."

By this time Jem was near the end of his dinner, for it was little that day, poor fellow, for he had the wife and eight children at home; and he was just going to peel his last potato, and little enough it was to give him till night at his work, when his little son, Billy (just four years old), comes running up the path, with his bright hair blowing in the wind, as pretty as you could see.

"Oh, what *will* I do with the childer, at all, when Father John curses me?" said Jem. And with that Billy runs up to him, crying, "Oh, daddy, daddy, gimme a praty."

"Be off out of that, you young thief," said Pat, "and don't be taking the dinner out of your daddy's mouth."

"Easy, Pat," said Jem; "sure if it was the

last praty I had in the world, or if I'd never eat a praty again, the darling would get it. Sure it's not one of them stones off the field I would be giving him."

And so Jem took Billy on his knee, and gave him the potato.

"Well, if that doesn't beat all," says Pat; "if them isn't a'most the very words of Jesus Christ himself."

"What words at all?" said Jem, quite surprised at what Pat said.

"What you said about the stone," said Pat. "Sure I read it in the Douay Bible on Sunday, the purtiest words that ever I saw in the book."

"And what were they at all?" said Jem.

"Why, I haven't just got the words," said Pat; "but I couldn't get the story out of my head, if I tried. Why, Jesus Christ himself was talking to all the people* about him, and teaching them the quietest and plainest way ever you heard. You would think it was the sweetest and quietest voice that ever spoke, to read them words. 'And,' says he, to all the people that was there, 'is there any one of you at all,' says

---

* Sermon on the Mount. Gospel of St. Matthew vii. 9 ; and Gospel of St. Luke xi. 11.

he, 'standing there, and if one of his little children would come and ask him for a bit of bread, is it a stone that you'd give him ? And if the likes of you,' says he, 'bad as you are, has that heart to your children, what must your Heavenly Father be to them that comes to ask of him ? Will he be any worse than you ?' Well, when I saw you give the last praty, Jem, to the poor child that I was hunting off you, it just came into my heart—Well, now, is that the way our Heavenly Father will do to one of us when we go to ask of him ?"

"Well," said Jem, "if them words doesn't teach me more about God than ever I knew before, or ever I learned from Father John ; and sure that *must* be true ; surely God *couldn't* be crosser or worse in himself to me, than the like of me is to the child, but a thousand times better. Sure, if that is not a thought to make us pray to him, and put our trust in him. I would rather hear them words, after giving Billy the praty, than all the words that ever I heard. Surely it *was* the Saviour that knew how to speak to poor people, and to teach their very hearts."

"That's just it, Jem," said Pat ; "and it's *that* that is making me take to the Bible. Sure, I expected, the first day I read it, to find it all about transubstantiation, and decalogues, and elephants,* and all kind of hard things that I don't understand ; and that every word of it would be disputing and argufying about everything, the way the Protestants and Catholics is always going on with each other ; and that there wouldn't be anything in it at all for poor people like me ; and, sure enough, I find a great deal that it isn't easy for me to understand ; but here and there I find some of the words of Jesus Christ himself, that's so plain and so loving, and that goes into my heart so easy and so sweet, that I can't help looking out for them words whenever I am reading ; and I wouldn't believe Father John, nor the bishop, nor the Pope himself, that them words could do me any harm, or be anything but good for me ; for, surely, Jesus Christ was fitter than the most learned of them all to give the right sort of teaching for poor and ignorant people ; and if Father John would only take and copy some of that teaching out of the Bible, it would be a different way with us."

"Well, now, I'll trust in God anyway for the praties," said Jem, "and I am not afraid now of

* Maybe Pat meant elements.

Father John or his curse, not even when I look
at Billy. Sure Father John told me to see what
the Bible could do for me; and sure I see it now!
To think now that I may go to my Heavenly
Father, just the way that Billy came to me; sure
that's more comfort than ever I had before this
day."

"And it's I that am glad that the words did
you good, Jem," says Pat; "and that same will
make me look for more words like them in the
same book; and, indeed, I'm thinking it's little
we know about the book, till we come to see how
it fits us in things like that. Them that is only
disputing about it, I'm thinking, knows nothing
of the good of it at all. I'm thinking now
there's hardly a thing that we poor people do,
that we won't find that Jesus Christ had some
words to say about that very thing; and sure
that's plain teaching for poor people anyway.
Why, as I was sitting at the door last Thursday
evening, reading my book, and the children play-
ing about, and they were on for hunting the
young chickens in spite of the wife, and there
was the old hen majoring about, and looking as
big and as grand as if she was fit to pick the
heads off them, and the children darn't go near

the chickens at all with her ; well, if I didn't
come in the very nick of time to a place in the
book (and sure enough I have, that marked)
where Jesus Christ says he only wants to gather
us together just the same as a hen gathers her
chickens under her wings, to take care of us the
way she does.* Sure that's making the very birds
teach us, and isn't that plain enough for anybody ?"

"Well, Pat," says Jem, "you're teaching me
the way to read ; and thank you kindly for it ;
and that's the way I'll read, for I was thinking
there was a deal I wasn't fit for, and no wonder,
considering how little the clergy ever instructed
us about it ; and now I'll look for what fits me,
and let Father John stop me if he can."

"Well, it's that I take to it for," said Pat; "and
I suppose there's something in the book for the
learned, and something for us, and that everybody may get their share ; and though I read a
good bit betimes, without coming to what is just
for the likes of me, yet when I get in, it's worth
the looking ; and maybe God meant just that
same, that we shouldn't get it without looking
for, no more than anybody will dig these praties

* Gospel of St. Matthew xxiii. 37.

without working for them first. And if it's his
will that we should get our bit by working for it,
and waiting for it, maybe it's just the same too
with our souls. Anyway I've got enough to
make me go on; and, with God's blessing, I'll
keep to the reading." And so the bell rung,
and Billy ran home, and we must wait till next
time.

CHAPTER V.

GOING TO HIMSELF.

WE hope our readers will be glad to hear what
Pat and Jem were talking about since. Well,
as they were walking home from their work, not
long since, Pat asked Jem, " What do you find in
the reading now, Jem ?"

" Why," says Jem, " my mind was running
on that story about the stone and the praty.
You mind what you told me about what our
Blessed Saviour said about it, and it made me
think so different of the great God from anything
I ever could think before, and it made me *feel*
so different like to him, that I took to reading
that place over and over. And sure if I had any
doubt about reading the Bible, the reading of

that story over and over makes me feel in my heart that reading God's book is a blessed thing to us, poor creatures. And then, when I was reading, the next verse stuck in my mind, and this is it—'Ask, and it shall be given to you; seek, and you shall find; knock, and it shall be opened to you. For every one that asketh receiveth; and he that seeketh findeth; and to him that knocketh it shall be opened.' And them words is in my mind, night and day; and there's something I understand, and something I don't."

" Well, tell us about that," says Pat.

" Well," says Jem, "I see plain enough about asking, for sure that is praying to our Father in heaven; and doesn't that say, that if we pray to him he will answer our prayers? And sure is not that the great thing for the like of us? Well, I see, too, about *seeking*. If we look to know God, we *will* come to know him; and where would we seek for him if we didn't in his own book? Sure I have found more about him *there* than ever I learned before; but there's one thing I can't make out at all, and that's about *knocking*—sure that would be at some gate or door like, that seemed closed agen us; but if we don't know *what the door is*, how can we get to knock at it ? and if we don't knock at it, how will we get it open ?   And I can't make it out at all, and I'm seeking for it, day and night, and thinking maybe will I find it if I seek."

"'Deed and I can help you then," says Pat, " and it's easy to find ; for sure I came on it last Sunday, when I was reading the 10th chapter of St. John's Gospel; and though I didn't take heed, as you did, to what our Saviour said about knocking, still I came on the answer."

" And what is it at all ?" said Jem.

So Pat repeated the verse (John, ch. x., v. 9, Douay Bible) where Christ says, "I AM THE DOOR ; by me if any man enter in he shall be saved."

" Well, if that isn't the very thing," said Jem ; " sure I'll never go to work at the squire's again without thinking of that.'

" And why so ?" said Pat.

" Don't you know," said Jem, " that big wall round the place, and how would I ever get in without the door in it ? and sure isn't that it entirely, when Christ says he's the door ? It means *the way in*, and that there's no stop when the door is open.   See the good now of our talking together on the road about the reading. One thing sticks to one person, and another to another; and when we put them together, just see how they fit!"

"Well that's true, anyway," said Pat; "but I doubt there's many a one striving to enter in by the Blessed Virgin and the Saints, and how will that be? Isn't that like making *her* the door? And, 'deed, I tried that long enough myself; for sure I never was told it was wrong, or got any teaching to learn me better, till I took to reading. But how will it be at all?"

"Is there anything about that in the Bible?" said Jem. "Is there anything in it at all for praying to the Blessed Virgin?"

"Well, I don't know," said Pat; "if it's in it I haven't come to it yet."

"Nor I, neither," said Jem; "nor nothing like it. But sure it's hard for me to say that it's *not* in the Bible; for there's a deal in it that I haven't read yet, and a deal more than what I have read; and how can I go to say that it isn't in that?"

"That's true enough," said Pat; "it's easy enough sometimes to know that a thing *is* in the Bible, but it's mighty hard for ignorant creatures

like us to know that a thing is *not* in the Bible.
If the priests would only teach us the Bible, and
show us what is in it and what isn't."

"Well, Pat," said Jem, "if the things *was* in
it, I suppose they would, and glad enough too ;
but if the things they teach us *isn't* in it, how
would it be expected they would tell us *that*, or
help us to know it ?   And that makes me think
there is things they teach us that isn't in the
Bible at all."

"Well, I mind now," said Pat, "that I heard
Father John preach a sermon against the Protestants, and he said they were heretics because
they did not pray to the Blessed Virgin and to
the saints and the angels.   And I mind he didn't
say it was in the Bible ; but still he showed us
the reason of it ; 'For,' says he, 'if you wanted
anything of the Queen, sure,' says he,' 'it isn't to
the Queen you would be going yourself,' says he,
' but you would try and get some one she cared
more about than she did about you ; and
wouldn't your own sense tell you,' says he, 'that
it would be better for you to get some great lord
or lady to speak for you, than to be putting
yourself on her ?'   Well, now," says Pat, "doesn't
all that stand to reason ?"

"Well, I mind that sermon, too," said Jem, "and I thought a deal of it then, but I don't now; for I was thinking it over since, and it doesn't stand to reason at all, when you come to look into it; for sure the Queen, God bless her, is only a woman like another, after all; and how could she have every one going to herself? Sure she would be fairly worried out of her life, if that was the way. Why, in the time of the famine, sure, that was so sore on us, was there man, woman, or child in this parish that wouldn't have gone straight to the Queen, God bless her, if they could only get at her? but how would it be with her, if all Ireland was going to her at wonst, to say nothing of England? Sure she could only talk to one at a time, just like any other; and that's the reason she must have other people for us to speak to, and to speak for us to her. But, sure, that isn't the way with God: sure, it couldn't put him out if all the people in the world were praying to him at wonst. So you see it doesn't agree at all, when you only come to look into it. And if I could go to the Queen at once, what would stop me? Sure if she was only *to see* little Billy, and him hungry, and asking me for a praty, when I had none to give him,

sure if she could only see that *herself*, wouldn't it
be better for me than if all the lords and ladies
in Ireland were talking to her about me? Sure,
don't we know that it's seeing that is believing?
Don't the quality hear enough about us, and the
distress that the poor is in? Sure, they see
enough of it in the newspapers to know all about
it, but that does no good; but if one of them
comes into our houses, and *sees* the want there,
then, sure enough, they give us help. So you see,
Pat, it's better for us always just to get to the
sight of them if we can, instead of leaving it to
others to tell them about us. Now, if God sees
what we want himself, and if he's able and
willing to hear us all, if we were all praying
together, without any trouble to himself, why
wouldn't we go to himself? Sure it doesn't
stand to reason at all, that because the Queen
can't see everything and speak to everybody herself, that God can't. And if matters is so different with God and the Queen, it's not common
sense for Father John to be telling us that our
own sense ought to make us to do to God what
has to be done to the Queen, only just because
she is like another body, and no greater in herself than one of ourselves. I would go straight

to her, *if I could;* and why wouldn't I go straight to God if I can ?"

"Well, Jem," said Pat, "there's reason in that, sure enough, only I didn't see it before ; and sure enough I would spake to the Queen afore the relieving officer or the inspector, if I could, and have more hope in it.   But how will we get to know at wonst if the Bible says anything about praying to the Virgin Mary, or getting her to offer our prayers to God, and to intercede with him for us ?   For I want to know that, and it would be long to wait till we get all the Bible read through."

"Well, that's what I want to know," said Jem, "and I can't be easy till I get the knowledge of it.   For sure the more I read in the Bible about God's goodness to them that ask him, the harder it seems not to know rightly the right way to ask him.   Sure I feel every day more and more, that it can't be right with me till I know how to pray to him in the way that it will please him to hear ; and the more I read about him, the more call I feel for praying to him in a way that I never did yet, and it's a hard case not to be sure of the right way."

Why wouldn't we ask Mr. Owens ?" said

Pat ; " sure he told us to go back to him any time we pleased, and we didn't go to him yet ; and why won't we ask him about this ?"

" Sure that's it," said Jem, " and it's early yet, and what's to hinder our just going down to him now ? maybe he will just show us what we want in the Bible, and settle us at once : sure enough let us try."

CHAPTER VI.

THE SAINTS AND THE ANGELS.

So Pat and Jem went straight to Mr. Owens's house, and he brought them into his study.

"Well, boys," said Mr. Owens, "did you read anything of the books, and how do you like them?"

"We like them well, your reverence," said Jem, "for they teach us more about God than ever we knew before, and they teach things that ought to make us love him, if we have any heart to him at all."

"And do you find much difference in the books?" said Mr. Owens, turning to Pat.

"Nothing to speak of, for so far, your reverence," said Pat; "there's words here and there not just the same; but for the *meaning*, there's no differ to signify, that I see yet."

"There are some differences, though," said Mr. Owens, "that will surprise you very much when you come to them, for some of them are just the very contrary of the difference you might expect to find in the two books. But I will tell you about that some other time, for I would rather hear you speak now, if you have anything to ask me about what you find in the books."

"That's just it, your reverence," said Jem; "we want to ask you about the right way of praying to God; for sure, when we see what he says to them that pray to him, it's a poor thing not to know the right way."

"Well," said Mr. Owens, "it's a good thing when reading the Bible makes us ask questions like that; but if you could explain your difficulty a little more, I might know better how to help you."

"Well, your reverence," said Pat, "we want to know if the likes of us poor creatures may just go straight to God and pray to him ourselves without anybody to speak to him for us; or if we must get somebody to speak for us and offer our prayers to him—somebody that he will be more willing to listen to than to ourselves."

"That's a very important question," said Mr. Owens, "and the answer is very plain; we are sinful and fallen creatures, not fit in ourselves to speak to a God who is of purer eyes than to behold iniquity; and therefore we have no reason to hope that our prayers will come up to him at all, unless somebody that a holy God can listen co should offer up our prayers to him, and intercede with him to accept our prayers."

"Why, your reverence," said Jem, "sure the Protestants don't believe that!"

"A man who does not believe that," said Mr. Owens, "cannot be a Christian, and so we need not talk about his being a Protestant; but we do believe it, and it lies at the root of our religion; and all our prayers to God are founded on it."

"And so," said Pat, "your reverence thinks it good to get the Blessed Virgin, and the angels, and the saints to speak for us to God, and get him to hear our prayers?"

"No," said Mr. Owens, "I did not say that we were to get *them* to speak for us; we should be sure to get some one that we know can hear us, and that we know God will hear."

"And who will we get, your reverence," said Pat, "if we don't get them to speak for us?"

"Maybe your reverence means," said Jem, "the verse that we read here in the two books the last night we were here."

"That's just what I mean," said Mr. Owens; "and now do you remember what it was?"

"I do, your reverence," said Jem; "it was just this—'There is one God, and one mediator of God and men—the man Christ Jesus.'"

"Well," said Mr. Owens, "we think that if we go to God without that mediator, that we have no right to believe that God will accept our prayers: but if we have that mediator to intercede for us, and offer up our prayers to God, and ask him to receive them, then our prayers will be accepted by God; and before we go any farther," said Mr. Owens, "let me show you out of the Douay Bible why we think so." So Mr. Owens turned to the following passages and read them—"'I am the way, and the truth, and the life; no man cometh to the Father but by me.'—John xiv. 6. 'Amen, Amen, I say to you, *if you ask the Father anything in my name* he will give it you.'—John xvi. 23. 'Jesus is entered into heaven itself, that he may *appear now* in the presence of God *for us.*'—Hebrews ix. 24 'He is able also to save for ever them that come to God by him; always living to make intercession for us.'—Heb. vii. 25. 'I have prayed for thee that thy faith fail not.'—Luke xxii. 32. 'And not for them (the Apostles) only do I pray, but for them also who through their word shall believe in me.'—John xvii. 20. So here you see," said Mr. Owens, "if we want to come to God in prayer we must come through Christ, who is the Way; and we must pray in the name of Christ if we want our prayers to be granted ; and then Christ makes intercession for us that our prayers may be heard ; and he prays *for* all who believe in his Word. So you see," said Mr. Owens, "we do not want for somebody to pray for us and to intercede with God to hear our prayers ; we have one who is able and willing to do it ; and if we want our prayers to be heard we must offer them up through his intercession— that is, we must ask him to speak for us and to offer our prayers to God."

" And may we ask the saints and angels to do it at all, your reverence ?" said Pat.

" That's a thing that God must know better than we can," said Mr. Owens. " I have showed you, out of the Douay Bible, that we have great promises to those who pray through Jesus Christ and ask him to intercede for them. But did you find in the Douay Bible any promise to those that pray through the Virgin Mary or the saints ?"

" Your reverence," said Jem, " that's the very thing we want to ask you ; neither of us has found the like of that in the Bible ; but we haven't read all the Bible, and it will take us long to do it, and maybe it is in that part that we haven't read ; and we just want to know if there

obtain mercy, and find grace in seasonable aid.'
—Hebrews ch. 4, v. 14 and 16. Here you see,"
said Mr. Owens, "our having such a High Priest
is sufficient to warrant us to pray *with confidence*
for the mercy and grace we want ; and if that
is enough to make us pray *with confidence*, what
room is there for anything more ? And more
than that," said Mr. Owens, "I can tell you,
that the Roman Catholic books that argue for
asking the saiuts to pray for us do never give any
proof for it out of the Bible ; and, of course, if
they could give proof out of the Bible they would."

"And what proof *do* they give for it, your
reverence ?" said Jem.

"The proof they give is this," said Mr. Owens:
"they say that the Bible tells us to pray for each
other, and to ask each other to pray for us. And
so far they are right, for the Bible does teach us
to do that ; and then they say, would it not be
better still to ask the angels and saints in heaven
to pray for us ? But that is an invention of their
own ; for the Bible does *not* say that."

"Well, your reverence," said Pat, "I would
like to hear more about that. Sure there's my
brother, that went to Australia, if he were here
now I would rather ask him to pray for me than

anybody at all.; he was the good brother, and he used to read the Bible betimes, afore any of the other boys thought of reading it ; and though he was not so attentive to his duties as some of them, he was the best Christian at all ; and sure I would be glad I could only ask him to pray for me ; and if he was in heaven, wouldn't he care for me still ? and wouldn't his prayers be better still ?"

"Well," said Mr. Owens, " I hope our friends in heaven do remember us, as we ought to remember them ; and it may be that they still pray to God for us ; but we can say nothing at all about that, because God has not told us anything about it ; and no one else could tell us anything about it. But I do not see how you, as a Christian, could ask your brother, in heaven, to pray for you, the same as you would if he was standing beside you."

" Well, if your reverence could show me the differ," said Pat.

" Where is he now ?" said Mr. Owens.

" In Australia, your reverence," said Pat.

" That is just at the other side of the world," said Mr. Owens ; "if you could make a hole straight down into the ground, and dig it about eight thousand miles deep, it might come out at

F

the other side, near about where he is ; it is a long way," said Mr. Owens.

"It is, your reverence," said Pat.

" And you would like to ask him to pray for you ?" said Mr. Owens.

" I would, your reverence," said Pat.

" Well, then," said Mr. Owens, "just go down on your knees here, this moment, and call on him to pray for you."

" Oh, your reverence," said Pat, "sure I couldn't do that."

" And why can you not do that ?" said Mr. Owens.

" Because, your reverence, he can't hear me," said Pat.

" Would it not be a great sin to do it ?" said Mr. Owens.

" It would, your reverence, not a doubt of it," said Pat ; "and I dursn't do it at all."

"But you would ask your brother to pray for you, if he were standing here beside you ?" said Mr. Owens.

" I would surely, your reverence," said Pat

" But it is quite a different thing to call on him to pray for you while he is in Australia ?" said Mr. Owens.

"It isn't like it at all, your reverence," said Pat.

" And if you got a letter to-morrow," said Mr. Owens, " to say your brother was dead, would that be the same as if he was standing here beside you ?"

" No, indeed, your reverence," said Pat ; " nothing like it."

" And if you then went down on your knees," said Mr. Owens, " and called on him to pray for you, which would that be most like—asking his prayers while he was standing beside you, or calling on him while he was in Australia ?"

" It would be a deal more like speaking to him while he was in Australia," said Pat.

" Well," said Mr. Owens, " the only reason the Roman Catholics can give for praying to the saints in heaven to pray for us is this, that it is just the same as asking our friends beside us to pray for us. Now, you see it is not the same, but quite different : it is just like praying to our friends on earth in a way that no Christian durst do, for fear of making God angry with us. Tell me now," said Mr. Owens, " would you go down on your knees and call on the present Pope, Pius the Ninth, who is at Rome, 1,000 miles off, to pray for you ?"

"No, your reverence," said Pat; "no Catholic would do that."

"Would it not be very wicked and sinful if they did?" said Mr. Owens.

"It would, your reverence," said Pat.

"Would it not be putting the Pope in the place of God, to suppose he could hear what you said?" said Mr. Owens.

"Well, I think it would be very like it," said Pat.

"If you spoke ever so loud the Pope could not hear you," said Mr. Owens.

"He could not, your reverence," said Pat.

"And if he knew of your prayer at all," said Mr. Owens, "it could only be because he knew the thoughts of your heart."

"Nothing else, your reverence," said Pat.

"Can you speak loud enough to be heard in heaven?" said Mr. Owens.

"I cannot, your reverence," said Pat.

"Well, then," said Mr. Owens, "if the saints hear your prayers, it can only be because they know the thoughts of your heart; and is not that putting them in the place of God, for Solomon says to God—' Thou only knowest the heart of all the children of men'?"　And here Mr.

Owens showed them the words in the Douay Bible—3 Kings, chap. viii., verse 39.

"And is there nothing in the Bible, your reverence," said Pat, "for praying to the saints or angels ?"

"Nothing at all," said Mr. Owens ; "and if there was, you may be sure Father John would show you that much of it ; but he would not like you to come upon these words of Jesus Christ—'*The Lord thy God shalt thou adore, and him only shalt thou serve.*' "—Matthew iv. 10.

"Well, your reverence," said Jem, "it now comes to my mind that I learned a catechism at the big school I learned to read in, that was kept by the monks, or the Christian Brethren, as they call them ; and in that catechism it was took out of the Bible that St. John, the Blessed Apostle, did worship an angel ; and sure St. John would not do it if it was wrong ; but I disremember what part of the Bible they took it out of."

"I will show you the catechism and the place in the Bible too," said Mr. Owens. So he took down off the shelf a little book, called "AN ABRIDGEMENT OF THE CHRISTIAN DOCTRINE, with proofs of Scripture, on points controverted, by way of question and answer. Composed in

1649, by H. T., of the English College at Douay. *Now revised by the* RIGHT REV. JAMES DOYLE, D.D., and prescribed by him to be used in the united Dioceses of Kildare and Leighlin. Dublin : Printed by Richard Coyne, 4, Capel-street, printer, bookseller, and publisher to the Royal College of St. Patrick, Maynooth, 1846." So Mr. Owens read out of the title page. " Is this the book ?" said Mr. Owens.

" It is, your reverence," said Jem ; "and is that the Doctor Doyle that was Roman Catholic Bishop of Kildare ?"

" The very man," said Mr. Owens, "and he was the most learned and clever man that has been a Roman Catholic bishop in Ireland for many years ; and you see he revised this book himself, and ordered it to be used in his diocess ; and that is the way you came to learn it. And now let us look for the Scripture proof for praying to angels, and you may be sure this book will give the best proof that can be got in the Bible." So Mr. Owens turned to page 52, where it speaks of the lawfulness of worshipping saints and angels. " Question—How prove you that ?" " Answer—First, out of Joshua, chap. v., verses 14 and 15, where Joshua did it—'I am Prince of the Host of the Lord, SAID THE ANGEL to Joshua, and Joshua fell flat on the ground, and adoring said, What saith my Lord to his servant?'" And here Mr. Owens bid them observe the words—"*Said the angel* to Joshua;" and then he turned to the place in the Douay Bible, and showed them that this person who spoke to Joshua is not called *an angel* at all, but, in the second verse of the next chapter, he is called THE LORD; so it was the Lord, and not an angel, that Joshua worshipped. And then Mr. Owens read the rest of the same answer in Dr. Doyle's Catechism. "Secondly, Apocalypse, chap. xxii., verse 8, *where St. John did it* (though the angel had once before willed him not to do it, in regard of his apostolical dignity, chap. xix, verse 10), ' And I fell down,' saith he, ' to adore before the feet of the angel, who showed me these things.'" And then Mr. Owens stopped; and Jem waited for a minute, and then he said—" And *did* the Blessed Apostle fall down to worship the angel?"

"He surely did," said Mr. Owens.

" And what does your reverence say to that?" said Pat ; " does not that make it out to be right to worship the angel ?"

So Mr. Owens said nothing at all; but he took

the Douay Bible, and opened it at the place that the catechism refers to (Apocalypse, or Revelation, xxii. 8), and bid Pat read it; and so Pat read—" And I, John, who have heard and seen these things. And after I had heard and seen, I fell down to adore before the feet of the angel, who showed me these things."

" Well, your reverence," said Pat, " is not that the very thing that is in the catechism ?" and Pat looked as if he thought now that Mr. Owens was only imposing on them, when he told them there was nothing in the Bible for worshipping angels, and that maybe the priests had the Bible on their side after all.

" And what do you say ?" said Mr. Owens, turning to Jem.

" What can I say," said Jem, " when St. John worshipped the angel ?"

" Read the next verse," said Mr. Owens to Pat.

So Pat read—" And *he* said unto me, SEE THOU DO IT NOT, for I am thy fellow-servant, and of thy brethren the prophets, and of them that keep the words of the prophecy of this book. ADORE GOD."

" You see now," said Mr. Owens, " when St.

John went to worship the angel, the angel warned him not to do such a thing, and told him to worship God."

"Well," said Jem, "if that does not beat all! Now I know what I wanted."

"What is that?" said Mr. Owens.

"That there is nothing in the Bible for worshipping angels," said Jem; "for sure, if there was any proof at all of it there, they would not have to go in such a barefaced like way to take a proof out of the very place that bids us not do it."

"That is enough for me, too," said Pat; "it's surely *not* in the Bible."

"One word more," said Mr. Owens. "You see in the note in the Douay Bible, on chap. xix., verse 10, it says, that maybe the angel only said it out of modesty, on account of the dignity of St. John as Apostle. That may lead you to think that though the angel was ashamed to let an apostle worship him, yet he would have let you or me adore him easy enough. So now, Pat, look back to the last verse you read, and see *why* the angel would not let St. John worship him."

"Because he was his fellow-servant, your reverence," said Pat.

was Mr. Nulty—a fine, free-spoken man, with a pleasant face, and a thriving man he is too. The other was old Mr. Barnes, who ought to be more of a gentleman than Nulty, for he was come of a good family in the country, and he had a property of his own that he farmed ; but he was a hard man, and what the Irish call "an ould nigger." And the two fell in on the road ; and Mr. Barnes began to grumble, "and it's enough to fret a man," said he, "so it is, to be giving them fellows twenty pence a day."

"Why," said Mr. Nulty, "I paid my men twenty-two pence yesterday, and I paid it willing." And so old Mr. Barnes stopped and faced round at Nulty.

" You have paid it willing ? " says he.

. " Yes, I did," said Mr. Nulty, "and I always do ; for I find that willing wages make willing men "

" Ay," said Mr. Barnes, "that's the way you're always raising the wages on us."

" I find it cheaper, as well as pleasanter," said Mr. Nulty, "and I'll bet you sixpence I had my reaping cheaper yesterday than you had."

So when they came to calculate, they found Mr. Nulty had got his reaping done one-and-sixpence an acre cheaper, at twenty-two pence, than Mr. Barnes had at twenty pence.

"I learned that from a farmer in England," said Mr. Nulty ; "he paid his men twelve shillings a week ; and when I came to count what his men did, I found he had his work done cheaper than I had here at tenpence a day : and since that, I find that better wages buys labour cheaper. And it stands to reason ; for if men find a fair advantage in being good labourers, they will strive to become better still. So I give a penny or two pence more than another, and get the best men ; and that makes them better still, and willing men into the bargain."

But Mr. Barnes only grumbled the more, and would not give in ; and when they were near the tree, Mr. Nulty stopped to speak to a neighbour, and Mr. Barnes went on to the tree, where Pat and Jem were standing among the boys. So Mr. Barnes said—"Boys, I'll give eighteen pence to-day, though it's a deal too much."

"Oh, sir," said Pat, "sure you would not be that hard on poor fellows that's often without work, and has nothing but the big tree to depend to."

"Well," said Mr. Barnes, "try if you can

"I mind, now," said Jem, "that I read that the harvest is the end of the world, and the angels are the reapers. But how could that be, that there were no labourers? Sure it can t mean that God has not angels enough to do what he wanted."

"It couldn't be that," said Pat; "but what can it be?"

So they turned it every way, and could make nothing of the harvest that wanted hands to cut it. And by this time they were at Mr. Nulty's field, for they walked fast.

"So," said Pat, "I wish I had my Bible with me, and we would try and make it out at dinner time.'

"Well I have mine," said Jem, "for it is small and handy, and fits in my pocket, so we will try it at dinner time."

And so they turned to, and did their best for Mr. Nulty. And as soon as they got through their dinner, Jem took out his Bible, and they began to look for it.

"I have it here," said Jem, "it's the last two verses of the 9th chapter of St. Matthew's Gospel;" and so he read—"Then saith he unto his disciples, the harvest truly is plenteous, but the labourers are few; pray ye therefore the Lord of the harvest, that he will send forth labourers into his harvest."*

"Now try," said Pat, "and find out where he was, and what he was doing, and then maybe we will see the meaning."

So Jem looked back a bit in the chapter. "I have that too," said Jem ; "he was preaching the Gospel (v. 35), and when he saw the great crowd of people he had compassion on them, because he saw they were like sheep that had no one to look after them ; and then he said it was a fine harvest, only the labourers was very few."

"Surely, then," said Pat, "the people was the harvest. But who were the labourers ?"

"Stay now," said Jem, "I see a mark in the side of the page to look to St. Luke (chap. x., verses 1, 2). And there they found that our Lord sent seventy of his disciples to go before him into every city, and tell the people about the kingdom of God (v. 9) ; and then he said to them (v. 2), 'The harvest truly is great, but the labourers are few.'"

* As Pat had not his Douay Bible at hand, we have compared all the verses in the two Bibles, and find the sense and meaning the same, only there is a little difference in some of the words.

"I see it now," said Pat. "The labourers were them that were to tell the people about Christ and the kingdom of God. Sure isn't it all plain now? Isn't there plenty of people in this field that knows as little about Christ as we did before we took to the reading? and maybe if any one would take the trouble to teach them, they would be as glad as ourselves to learn, for sure there is a deal of the boys that's not satisfied with Father John's ways, and that would be willing to learn better: and wouldn't that be the fine harvest? And isn't it the harvest that's losing for want of men to save it?"

"Well, if that isn't true," said Jem; "but where's the labourers? I wonder how it would be if the readers, that I hear is about Ballycarney, was to come down this way and try the people here. But sure enough that sort of labourers is few."

"'Deed and I think there is many would listen to them ready enough," said Pat, "if they came into their houses, in a quiet way, of an evening."

"And couldn't we get some of the neighbours to read with ourselves of an evening?" said Jem.

"Why, then, I think we might, easy enough,"

said Pat, "and a good thing it would be ; but, then, wouldn't Father John soon come to hear of that, and wouldn't he destroy us entirely ?   Why, even Mr. Nulty would hardly dare to employ us, if Father John was to give orders against it on the altar."

" Why, then," said Jem, " if the biggest thistle in Ireland was standing fornint me to-day, I wouldn't stop reaping for fear of pricking my fingers ; and if ever we put our hand to Christ's harvest, we will have to face the thistles too ; and if we go on reading ourselves, it will come to that sooner or later ; and maybe, as Mr. Nulty says of double work, the sooner the better."

" Ay," said Pat, " there's a verse that troubles me often of late, where our Saviour says, that if we are ashamed of him before men, he will be ashamed of us before the angels of God ; and, sure, that should make us face thistles and all. But do you think," said Pat, " that we will ever see such a harvest of people in Ireland ?"

" It's my opinion," said Jem, " it's coming fast ; and if the readers come down this way you'll see."

So the bell rung, and they were off to their work ; and when evening came, Mr. Nulty paid

them two shillings and twopence a man, for he
always gave the height of the wages, and a little
more ; and very thankful his men were, and so
was Mr. Nulty, for not a man in the parish had
his reaping as cheap by the acre that day.

CHAPTER VIII.

THE READERS IN KILCOMMON.

" Oh, Jem, where have you been all this time ?"

" Why, Pat, I got a job down to Roscommon, to drive up some cattle, and I only got back last night," said Jem.

" Well, it's I that's wishing to have a talk with you, Jem," said Pat.

" And what is it about ?" said Jem.

" Why, sure the readers is come !" said Pat.

" And where are they come ?" said Jem.

" Why, into the very town of Kilcommon itself," said Pat.

" Well," said Jem, " if that doesn't beat all ! Didn't I think, if ever they came down this way, it would be in some quiet, out of the way place like this they would come, where, maybe, some of us would let them in of an evening unknownst ; but what will they do in Kilcommon at all ?"

" Well, then, it's there they've come," said Pat, " right into Father John's mouth, and facing all the blackguards in Kilcommon ; and of all the work ever you see it's in Kilcommon it is."

" Tell us all about it : will you ?" said Jem.

after them a bit ; and so I went to see what they were doing, and sure enough they were walking about as bold as you please, and a real clergyman with them, and he with his Douay Bible in his hand, saying, he only wanted to tell the people what was in that, and that if he met Father John he would hold his own tongue, and only hand the book to Father John, and ask him to read some of that and explain it to the people. And sure enough I didn't wonder that Father John kept out of the street he was in, for that would be new work for Father John."

"Well, and how did it end at all ?" said Jem.

"Why, it just went on the same way till Saturday," said Pat ; " the readers getting into all the houses quite pleasant, for no one liked to put them out, and Father John running about at the far end of the town, for fear he would meet them ; and so it went on till Saturday night. Well, on Sunday morning, says I to myself, I'll just go into the chapel at Kilcommon (where I wasn't, sure enough, for long enough), and I'll hear what Father John has to say about it. Well, of all the scolding and cursing that ever you heard a priest give at the altar it was the terriblest. First he fell on the Ranters, and the

Swaddlers, and the Soupers, and the Jumpers, and the unbaptized heathens, and the cockatrices, and the goose-stealers, and a deal more names he had for them ; and, sure enough, I wondered why he called them goose-stealers (for them's as decent men as you would see, more like gentlemen than Father John, with all his bad language), till I saw him turn round to some old women that were in the chapel, and says he, ' Now you old women there, mind you look after your geese,' says he, 'for these Soupers are so fond of soup,' says he, ' that when the bacon's out, it's stealing your geese they'll be,' says he, ' to make soup of.' Well, thinks I to myself, says I, if that's all you have to say against reading the Bible, the readers will have the town yet, thinks I ; and with that he went on to Mr. Owens for fetching the readers, and of all the bad names that ever was called he had the baddest for him. ' And,' says he, ' when the cholera was in Ireland, their clergy,' says he, ' that's married and has wives,' says he, ' all presented a petition to the Protestant bishop,' says he, ' that they mightn't go to the cholera hospital,' says he ; ' but let the Protestants die like dogs,' says he. And thinks I to myself that's enough, any way ; for when I was lying ten days in the and when that was tired with the other hand, at the other ear, screeching himself black in the face ; and then the clergyman would say, holding up the Douay Bible in his hand—' Is it your own Bible that you hate, that you treat it that way ? Why don't your priest come himself, and show if the book is a bad one ?'   And, indeed, when the people saw how pleasant and quiet the readers behaved, they thought it bad work, and out comes old Sally Smith, and says she to the jammer, ' Is that what you're at, and isn't it yourself that would sell the priest next for a glass of whisky ?'   And, indeed, I heard, after that, that the jammer was hired by Father John, and that he had a pound to put the readers out of Kilcommon, and no cure no pay.   But that's the way it is ; and what will come of it I don't know at all."

" Well, Pat," said Jem, " I'm thinking that if the priest has nothing to say agen the Bible but dirty water, and mud, and shouting, and the ringing of a bell, he'll never put it out of Kilcommon that way.   Sure all the boys must see, when they come to think of it, that their religion is in a bad way when the priest has nothing else to say for it."

" Well, indeed, I'm thinking that's true," said Pat ; " but we'll see, and who knows but the readers and the Bible will have Kilcommon yet ?"

CHAPTER IX.

THE CONTROVERSIAL CLASS.

" Well, Pat, I thought long to see you, to get the news of Kilcommon ; how is it at all ?

" Well, it's bad enough, Jem, and it's good enough, too," said Pat.

" And how's that, Pat ?" said Jem ; " tell us all about it."

" Well, it's bad enough with Father John, stirring up all the blackguards ; you never saw the like ; any dacent man would be ashamed of it; but Father John is ashamed of nothing. The readers was covered with mud, and half kilt with stones a dozen times ; but some of the boys got put up for that, so matters is easier that way now, at least in the town ; but if the readers go out into the country parts, there's enough to set on them as if they were mad dogs; but that is not the worst ; it's the bad words of a deal of these people that makes me think worse of the teaching the people has been getting than any-

"Well, I will," said Pat; "sure Mr. Owens and the missioner—that's the Rev. Mr. Burke that's come—has opened what they call a controversial class : it's a meeting where everybody may come, and talk, and argue, and question, as much as they like, and Mr. Owens and Mr. Burke to answer them all."

"Well, and does any Catholics go ?" said Jem.

"A deal of them," said Pat.

"And how do they behave there ?" said Jem

"Oh, quite dacent and proper," said Pat ; "for no one goes there that Father John can stop ; and though there's some that's mighty earnest for their own way, and thinks they can puzzle any clergyman at all, yet they're not under Father John's thumb, or they wouldn't be there ; so they argue quite fair and clever ; and Mr. Burke and Mr. Owens answers them so fair and so kind, that they're well pleased, even when they're beat ; and it's the pleasantest and the hamperedest plan at all."

"And what do they talk about ?" said Jem.

"Why, the last night," said Pat, "they were talking about mortal and venial sin.　And first, Mr. Owens says, says he, 'Is there anything in the Douay Bible,' says he, 'to show that there is any such difference as mortal and venial in the nature of sinful actions ?'   ' Sure there is,' says Phil Dooley, who is a mighty good scholar, and has bought a Douay Bible to bring with him. 'And where is it ?' says Mr. Owens. So Phil Dooley opened his Bible and read—'He that knoweth his brother to sin a sin which is not to death, let him ask, and life shall be given to him who sinneth not to death. There is a sin unto death.'—1 John v. 16.   So Phil looked quite satisfied, and was going to shut the book."

" Stop a minute," said Mr. Burke ; "just read the note on that in the Douay Bible."

So Phil read—" It is hard to determine what St. John here calls a sin which is not to death, and a sin which is unto death.   The difference CANNOT be the same as betwixt sins that are called venial and mortal."

" That will do," said Mr. Burke.   " I thought the Church of Rome had the true interpretation of Scripture, but it seems they find it hard to interpret this ; but they are agreed with us that this verse does *not* mean the difference between mortal and venial sin, and that is enough for what we are at to-night.   But can any one show anything else about it in the Douay Bible ?" says he.

And no one had anything to say.

" No wonder," said Mr. Owens, "for there is nothing in the Douay Bible about it; but can any one tell me how they learned anything about it, when it's not in the Bible ?"

" Sure I learned it in the catechism," said Peter Foley.

" And what catechism did you learn ?" said Mr. Owens.

" Plunket's Catechism," said Peter Foley.

" How many chief kinds are there of mortal sin ?" said Mr. Owens.

" Seven, called capital sins," said Peter Foley.

" Which are the seven called capital sins ?" said Mr. Owens.

" Pride, covetousness, lust, anger, gluttony, sloth," said Peter Foley.*

" Turn to Apocalypse, ch. xxi., last half of the 8th verse," said Mr. Owens.

So Foley read—"All liars, they shall have their portion in the pool burning with fire and brimstone."

" Is lying a mortal sin ?" said Mr. Owens.

" Well, it must be," said Foley, "if liars will go to hell."

* Plunket's Catechism, pp. 22 and 23.

" Which of the seven mortal sins is it ?" said Mr. Owens.

" Well, it's not among them in the catechism," said Foley.

" Is idolatry a mortal sin ?" said Mr. Owens.

" Surely it is," said Foley.

" Which of the seven is it ?" said Mr. Owens.

" Well, it's not among them either," said Foley.

" Well," said Mr. Owens, " it seems dangerous to trust in that catechism, for fear we might come under the judgment of God for mortal sins that are not among the seven. Now," says Mr. Owens " can you tell me, out of the catechism, what is venial sin ?"

" A less offence to God, which does not deprive us of sanctifying grace nor deserve hell,"* said Foley.

" And can you tell me, out of the catechism, what sort of things are venial sins ?" said Mr. Owens.

" No," says Foley, " that's not in it," says he.

" Well, I think it might," said Mr. Owens, " if it's of such consequence to know the differ."

* Plunket's Catechism, p. 23.

"I can tell it, your reverence, for it's in mine," said Peter Dooley.

"Oh, you learned Dr. Doyle's Catechism, or the Christian Doctrine," said Mr. Owens.

"I did, your reverence," says Peter, "and here it is—'A venial sin, for example, *a vain word*, an officious jesting lie, the theft of a pin or an apple.'"

"Does the Douay Bible tell us that vain words are venial sins?" says Mr. Owens.

"It does not, your reverence," says I, "for the Douay Bible tells us, in Matthew xii. 36, that Christ himself said—'I say unto you, that every idle word that men shall speak they shall render an account for it in the day of judgment.'"

"Very good," says Mr. Owens. "Now take the next. Does the Douay Bible say that any lies are venial sins ?"

"Well, we had that already," said Peter Foley —"'ALL LIARS shall have their portion in 'the pool burning with fire and brimstone ;' that, surely, is hell : so there is no use in saying that any liars are only guilty of venial sin."

"Now take the third," says Mr. Owens. "Does the Douay Bible say that stealing apples is a venial sin ?"

"Well," says Daly, the schoolmaster, "if it wasn't Eve taking an apple, or the likes, that brought sin and death into the world."

"Quite right," says Mr. Owens; "and now," says he, "look to your catechisms, and look to your own souls, if you trust to catechisms, that tell you these three things are venial sins that cannot break charity between God and man, when the Douay Bible tells you that these three things bring men under death, judgment, and hell"

And with that Mr. Burke says—"One word, boys, before we stop. What is sin ?" Well, now, doesn't it seem a mighty easy question ? and yet, no one had an answer ! So Mr. Burke opened the Douay Bible, at 1 John, chap. iii., verse 4, and read—"Whosoever committeth sin committeth also iniquity; and *sin is iniquity*." "Now," says he, "can a man commit sin at all without committing iniquity ?" So he put it all round to the boys, and all allowed that was plain, for "Whosoever committeth sin committeth also iniquity." "Well," says Mr. Burke, "if a man commits a venial sin does he commit sin or not ?" So all the boys allowed that he does. "And does he commit iniquity ?" says Mr. Burke. So was knocked off, and their heads cut, and lumps on them as big as eggs. And then the polis comes down, and takes Paddy Brady, and Mick Dooly, and another that was foremost, and marches them off. 'And sure,' says the boys, 'it's only defendin' our religion we are.'"

"And arn't they the pretty fellows to be defendin' their religion ?" said Jem.

"Sure enough," said Pat, "I believe it's little they trouble the priest about religion. I hear tell there's not one of them has been at confession these five years ; but Father John thinks them the right sort now, as you'll find."

"Well, on the Friday after, the boys were to be tried afore the bench, and it happened to be a holiday, so there was no work doing ; and I seen such a crowd going to the chapel that I went there, too, to hear what Father John would say ; and, sure enough, after Mass, the sermon was all about the firebrands, and the soupers, and the ranters, and the poor, innocent boys that was going to be tried, and persecuted, and exterminated, only just for trying to keep their religion from being insulted by the firebrands. So when he was tired, says he, 'Now go down every one of you,' says he, 'man, woman, and child,' says he, 'and stand by the poor fellows that's going to be persecuted and swore against by the fire-brands,' says he.   So sure enough, when I got to the courthouse, there was a thousand people there anyway.   And there was Mr. Foley, the lawyer, from Dublin, come down to defend the boys."

"And who paid for his coming?" said Jem.

"Why," said Pat, "Father John sent round his servant, and two or three of his head men, to all the Catholic shopkeepers and tradesmen in Kilcommon, and made them all subscribe their pounds, and ten shillings, and five shillings ; and I heard tell they liked it little enough, but they were mostly all afraid to bring Father John's tongue on them in the chapel ; only Mr. Nulty and one or two more that never cares what Father John can say.   Well, the readers told their story mighty fair and clever, and then Mr. Foley got up and examined them, to make them confess they were insulting the people, and he fetched out a tract, and asked them did they give any of that ; and they said they did a few ; and then he read out a place where it said the priests was

it was it would be paid.   And while I was wondering where the like of them would get the
money, I turned round, and saw Father John
with his roll of bank notes out in his hand."

" Ay," said Jem, " I seen that myself, after the
work at the election last summer, when Father
John paid down the money in open court for
every one of the boys that was fined for the work
—and a bad work it was.*   But did the magistrates let them off with a fine ?"

" 'Deed didn't they," said Pat, " this time.
Old Mr. Everards says, just as quiet and easy as
you please—'It's a month's imprisonment and
labour we're going to give them,' says he.   And
I never seen Father John look so mad, for he
wasn't going to stand *that* for the boys.   Still it's
a pretty good thing they made of it ; for all their
wives and children got new clothes, and meal,
and money, and what not."

" And isn't that the dacent way for Father
John to be defending his religion ?" said Jem ;
" didn't the Rev. Mr. Owens write him a letter,
asking him to settle who was right, by fair discussion, before the people ?   But Father John
would rather get his religion defended with

* Jem is quite correct about this fact, too.

stones and mud, by the blackguards that never comes to confession at all : and doesn't all that show who knows that he has fair reason on his side ?"

"Well, Jem," said Pat, "I am coming to think more and more that the priests hasn't reason on their side, and that they know that, once it comes to fair argument, the people will find out that. But as I was going home I fell in with Mr. Owens, and had a talk with him. 'And,' says he, 'why wouldn't we be stoned,' says he, 'when the blessed Apostles was stoned in almost every place they went to preach in ?' says he, and with that he pulled out his Bible, and showed me two places where the Apostles was stoned for speaking to the people ;* and another place where the Jews gathered up all 'the wicked men of the vulgar sort, and made a tumult, and set the city on an uproar,'† just for all the world the way Father John does now, 'and so it's no new thing,' says he, 'but we must follow the way the blessed Apostles went.'"

"But, your reverence," says I, "what can poor men like the likes of us do when the priest can get up the like of that agin any of us, and

* Acts xiv 5 and 19.   † Acts xvii 5.

much as any of us.' 'Ay, that's the reason of it,' says Mr. Smith, 'and that's always the way; whatever's their convenience is our duty; and f I'd only known that this morning,' says he, 'I'd have had every plough in Kilcommon at work.'* 'And why shouldn't we work to-day, and the work so backward?' said Mr. Nulty; 'ne'er a priest in Ireland should stop me to please himself.'"

So then Pat and Jem had some talk about why Lady-day could not be kept on the 25th of March, because it was Good Friday; but we need not tell what they said about that, because we see one Brannigan has written a letter about it.

"And then," says Jem, "I wonder did God Almighty mean that the priests should be laying down laws for us to work, or not to work, just as suits their own convenience and their own crop."

" Well," says Pat, " if he did, wouldn't he put it in the Bible, or wouldn't the blessed Apostles say something about it?   And there isn't a word about it in the Bible that I can find; and sure, if it *was* in the Bible, wouldn't the priests tell us that much out of the Bible anyway?   But I know what is in the Bible—that we are not to

* Such a conversation did take place between two farmers on that day, who lived in different parish s.

work on the Sabbath-day, and we are given leave to work on the other six."

"Ay," said Jem, "it's not much the priests seem to think about that ; sure there isn't a shop in Ballyboy that isn't open on Sunday ("and it's worse in Kilcommon," said Pat) and every one doing his business ; and the publicans busier nor any other day selling their whisky ; and how can it be right for the publican to be selling his whisky and doing *his* business, any more than for the farmer to be sowing his ground, and doing *his ?* And who ever heard tell of a priest saying it was against the law of God for a shop-keeper to be doing his business on Sunday ? But if any one of *us* goes to earn a shilling on a holyday, to keep the children from dying of hunger, they are ready enough to tell us that it's against the law of the Church, and to put their curse upon us, and to take the bread out of the children's mouths for it ; for who will give us a day's work when they do that on us ?

"Well," said Pat, "and isn't it what they would do ? Sure it's to think of the Church, and not of the Scriptures, that they want us ; and why wouldn't they be harder on us about the laws of the Church, that they make themselves, than about the laws of God, that he wrote in the Bible ? But I wonder which will be most thought of in the day of judgment, whether we kept the laws of God himself or the laws of the priest."

"Well, then," said Jem, "if God's to be the judge, maybe he will think most about his own laws.   And if that's to be the way, isn't it better for us to read the Bible now, and find'out his laws for ourselves, if the priest is too busy about his own, to tell us what God's laws are ?

"Well, Jem," said Pat, "I'm thinking we'll have to keep to the Bible to know *them ;* and sure enough, that's just what I came to talk to you about.   Do you mind what I said to you the last talk we had, how the Rev. Mr. Owens asked me would I be ashamed of Christ and of his Word ; and would I make Christ be ashamed of me ? and what he showed me in the Bible about it ?   Well, I couldn't get it out of my head at all; and it was turning up in my mind every minute, that if I met Father John I'd be ashamed of Christ's Word, and that Christ would be ashamed of me, and I couldn't tell what I would do at all.   Well, I was walking along the road on Saturday, think- ing what would I do at all if Father John taxed

me with reading the Bible; and while I was
studying it, who should come up but Father John
riding along, and when he saw it was me, he just
pult up along side of me, quite sudden. 'Is that
you?' says he. 'It is, your reverence,' says I ;
and, indeed, it's I that would be glad to say that
same time that it wasn't. 'And what are you
doing now?' says he. 'I'm working with Mr.
Connor, of Kilcommon,' says I. 'That's not
what I mean,' says he; 'you know what I mean,'
says he ; 'what are you doing now?' says he.
Well, I didn't know what to say, and I hadn't a
word in me at all, good nor bad ; and says he,
shouting at me, that it would make you afeard to
hear him, 'Is it reading the Bible you are?' says
he. Well, it just came in my mind that minute
—would I be ashamed of Christ's own Word, and
would I make him ashamed of me ? and my mind
was just riz in me that minute, and so I up and
I told him, 'It is, your reverence,' says I, 'reading the Bible,' says I. Well, with that he got so
angry you never saw Father John so like himself
in all your life ; now, you never seen a man so
boisterous. And when his reverence got something easy within himself, with letting it out, he
says to me, says he, 'And it's the heretic Bible

you're reading, going to turn heretic,' says he.
' No, indeed, your reverence,' says I ; 'it isn't
the heretic Bible, it's only the Douay Bible,' says
I.   ' And where did the likes of you get a Douay
Bible ?' says he.   'I got it from the Rev. Mr.
Owens,' says I.   ' And what business has the
likes of him giving you the Douay Bible ?' says
he ; ' why didn't he give the heretic Bible ? like
a heretic, as he is,' says he.   'It's ranter your
turning,' says he.   'No, please your reverence,'
says I, 'I don't rant none ; and sure, your reverence,' says I, 'the Douay Bible would not
make ranters of us,' says I.   'It's a swaddler
you are,' says he, 'and a jumper, and it's to the
soup-kitchen you're going,' says he, 'and to hell ;
and its spiritual prostitution,' says he, 'and it's
taking bribes you are, and selling your faith,
and your soul, and your God,' says he, ' for base
lucre.   But I'll be up to you now,' says he ; " I'll
just give you your choice,' says he ; ' there's the
Bible and there's me,' says he, 'and which of us
can do you most harm ?' says he ; 'so now make
your choice—will you have me or the Bible,'
says he, ' or will you give up the Bible, or will
you give up me ?' says he.   Well, now, I felt in
myself that I was getting bolder and bolder all

the time he was talking, and so, when he left a bit of room for me to put in a word, I just says to him, says I, 'Since your reverence is so good as to give me my choice,' says I, 'I think I'll just stick to the Bible,' says I. Well, with that he took on so that you wouldn't believe; and just then there was a parcel of the Kilcommon boys coming up the road, and he just turns to them, and says he, 'This is a souper,' says he, 'and a ranter, and a swaddler,' says he, 'and a jumper,' says he, 'and Judas that sold his soul for soup,' says he, 'and denied his God here to my face,' says he. 'No, indeed, your reverence,' says I, 'I got no soup at all, nor nothing else, nor I don't mean to look for any, nor take it if it was offered to me, and indeed it was not,' says I. 'Well, it's going to be a turncoat you are,' says he, 'that none of your people was before.' 'Indeed, I'm not, your reverence,' says I, 'if you don't put me out, and turn me yourself; but sure,' says I, 'your reverence won't put me out and turn me only for reading the Catholic Bible,' says I; 'sure don't the Catholic bishops say, in the first page of it, that it's good for Catholics to read, and sure, your reverence, it can't make anything bad of me; and so your reverence,' says I, 'may as well just let me alone for reading it, and it's not going to turn at all I am,' says I. But he didn't listen to me at all, but just went on to the boys ; and with that they set up a shout after me, that you would hear from that to this, and called me all that Father John called me, and more foreby ; and it's I that was glad, when I came to a bit of loneing, to try to get out of their way as far as I could ; and ever so far I'd hear them shouting ranter, and souper, and jumper, and Judas, after me, that you never heard the like."

"Well, Pat," said Jem, "you're in for it now anyway ; but it's my opinion, if you can only hold out for a while, you'll have a deal of the boys, and myself too, to keep you company."

So if we hear more of what goes on in Kilcommon, maybe our readers will like to know it.

CHAPTER XII.

THE WAKE.

"WELL, Pat, did you get leave to stay in Kilcommon?" said Jem, when they met on the road.

"'Deed I did, then," said Pat, "and it's peace we are getting in Kilcommon now."

"And how is that come about?" said Jem.

"Why, I hear tell," said Pat, "that Father John got a letter from the Bishop, telling him he was bringing scandal on the Church, and that everything is to be kept quiet till it's forgot."

"And you're not going to turn, Pat?" said Jem.

"'Deed no, Jem," said Pat; "sure I was never thinking of turning; what do I know about it? Sure I only want to read the Catholic Bible, and try to learn something out of it.   But where were you, Jem, since I saw you?"

"Why, then, I was at the wake," said Jem.

"And whose wake was it?" said Pat.

"Well, then, it was old Molly Kearney's," said Jem.

"Is it her, the creature?" said Pat; "and

where would the likes of her get a wake ?   Sure,
don't I know that she had nothing to live on
these ten years only the fifteen pence a week that
Mr. Owens allowed her out of the Church money,
and she give three pence a week of that for her
lodging, and who would be bothered waking her ?
'Deed, Mrs. Owens was mighty good to her, and
gave her her bit often ; but sure Mr. Owens
wouldn't be going to pay for the pipes and
whisky ?"

"Well, you may say that," said Jem ; "but
I'll tell you how it was.   I was going past old
Ned Flanagan's, where she lodged, one evening,
and he called me in, and told me she was dead,
the creature ; and he said he wasn't going to have
any nonsense of waking, only just what was
wanting ; and so he asked me to go down to the
shop, at the cross roads, for two halfpenny candles, and a pen'orth of snuff, and he said that
would do.   So I went, and got the candles and
the snuff ; and when the candles was lighted,
who should come in but old Judy Brannigan,
that has the Scapular, and sells the books ; well,
down she goes on her knees, you know, and
begins with the Latin, and 'deed she seemed to
handle it mighty clever ; and when she was done,

'Judy, dear,' says I, 'what is it at all?' 'Well, I b'lieve it's a Psalm,' says she; 'but I'm sure it's the right thing,' says she. 'And, Judy, dear,' says I, 'do you know what it means at all?' says I. 'How would I,' says she, 'when it's in the Latin it is?' 'And what is it good for?' says I. 'Why, it's good for old Molly Kearney's soul,' says she. 'And wouldn't it be good for our souls, too?' says I. 'Well, in course it would,' says she. 'And would the meaning of it do any harm to them that understood it?' says I. 'No, sure it wouldn't,' says she. 'Well,' says I, "and wouldn't it be better for us to have it in English, the way we could understand it?' 'And is it jumper you're going to turn?' says she, 'to be talking that way of the blessed Latin; sure where would be the use of larnin' at all, if English was as good for the soul as Latin?' 'Well, I'm thinking, Judy,' says I, 'our souls wouldn't be the worse for understanding good words.' So, with that, old Ned Flanagan comes over, and he says, ''Deed, I'm thinking this long time there's sense in that,' says he; 'and I can't help thinking, betimes, where's the great use in my going to Mass, when I can't understand one word, good nor bad, till the scoulding begins?' "

"Ay," says Pat, "that's the sarmon he meant, sure enough ; and I wonder what's the reason they don't scould in Latin, too.   Sure, if we listen to the prayers in Latin, why wouldn't it do to listen to the scoulding in Latin too ?   It's a poor way with us to understand nothing but the scoulding ; it ought to make us read the Bible anyway, to try and know something—but go on with the story, Jem."

"Well," said Jem, " when old Judy saw that we were both again her, she began taking a pinch of the snuff ; and I says, 'Isn't it you that has the blessed Scapular, Judy ?' says I   ''Deed, it's myself,' says she, 'that has.'   'And what is it good for ?' says I: ' Why, it's good to die in, to be sure,' says she, 'and it's I that hopes to get it on in time,' says she, 'if my senses is spared to me,' says she.   'And what's the good of dying in it ?' says I.   ' Why, to be sure,' says she, ' don't you know ?   Didn't the Blessed Virgin say herself, when she gave it, that them that dies in it shall never go to hell, and if they go to purgatory at all, that she'll go down there herself the very next Saturday after they die, and let them out herself ?' ' And where did you hear that at all ?' says I ; 'is it in the Bible it is ?'   'Sure, how would I know if it's there?' says she; 'but isn't it in the treatise on the Scapular that I have at home?' says she. 'And you won't put it on till you are dying?' says I. 'No,' says she, 'sure I won't.' 'And how will it be,' says I, 'if you wouldn't have the sense to put it on then?' says I; 'sure here's old Molly Kearney lying here,' says I, 'and she wasn't as old as you, and she was took quite sudden, and if she had a dozen Scapulars in her box, would it be any good to her soul, when she wouldn't have time or senses to put one of them on her?' Well, now, the creature, I was a most sorry for saying it, when I saw how troubl'd she got in her mind at thinking of that. 'Oh, wirra,' says she, 'won't there be any good Christian near me at all to put it on me? Ochone,' says she, 'will I die with the Scapular in the chest, at the foot of the bed there?' Well, when I saw the old creature take on so, I just says to her, 'Did you never hear, Judy dear,' says I, 'that it's in the Bible, that the blood of Jesus Christ cleanseth us from all sin? and sure,' says I, 'if he will put that on you his ownself, there will be no mistake about that; and won't that do?' says I. 'Och,' says she, 'what do I know about that, but don't I know about the blessed

Scapular ? but, ochone,' says she, 'who will put it on me at all ? sure, I'm a poor lone creature, that lives by myself, without kith or kin, and who will put it on me at all ?' Well, I couldn't help thinking that time, that it was the poor case for an old creature to be taking such trouble about her soul, and knowing nothing of the blood of Jesus Christ to put away her sins ; and isn't it the poor thing for the priests to be leaving an old creature that way, that will be dying like old Molly some of these days ? And don't they all hold up poor Judy for the most religious woman in the country, and the surest of heaven ? Well, it makes me think more nor ever that reading the Bible is what the people want.

"Well, but while I was talking to old Judy, there came a noise at the door, and when it opens, there was all the wildest boys in the country coming in ; and old Ned Flanagan goes for'ed to meet them, and—'What do you want here ?' says he. 'We're come to the wake,' says they. 'Well, you'll get no waking here,' says he ; 'so you may be off with yourselves.'   Well, they swure they'd have some of the fun over old Molly : 'And what did you or the likes of you care for old Molly when she was living ?' says he ; 'and

what right have you to fun over her now ?' says
he ; 'so be off with yourselves out of that,' says
he.   Well, with that they gave him a deal of bad
language, and they pushed by him, and drove
into the house, and began screeching for the
pipes and the whisky, for they said they had a
right to have some divarsion when there was a
corp in the house.   Well, that old Ned
went up into the inner room, and he fetched out
his scythe with him (for he's a mower by trade),
and he swure—'By this and by that,' says he,
' if they didn't be off with themselves out of that,'
says he, 'he'd shear the heads off of them, like
mice,' says he.   Well, 'deed if I hadn't caught
hold of his arm, I think he'd have had the arm
off one of them anyway ; and when the boys saw
that, they weren't long in being off with themselves.

" Well, when they were gone, says I to Ned,
' Would you let me read a bit quiet to you ?'
says I.   So he said he'd like that well ; so I just
took out my Bible, for I had it in my pocket,
and I just read to them about Jesus Christ
coming to Mary and Martha when their brother
was dead, and how kind he was to them, and how
he even cried like themselves at the grave ; how

and the Bible—that is, barring it isn't all a lie about the Scapular. But, I'm thinking, if the Bible is true, it will go hard with poor Judy and them that trusts in this book."

"Well, what is it all about?" said Pat.

"Why, first and foremost," said Jem, "it tells us how the order of Carmelites was founded by Elijah the prophet, on Mount Carmel (p. 12); and it tells us how he was upon the mountain nine hundred years and more before our Saviour was born, and he seen a little cloud, as big as his hand, coming up out of the sea, and that was the Blessed Virgin herself, no less ! and so then he set up the Carmelites in honour of her, and it tells the place in the Bible where to find it (3rd Book of Kings, ch. xviii., v. 44, &c., Douay Bible ; 1st Book, authorized version) ; and sure enough, when I went to look for it, Elijah was there, and saw the little cloud, but not one word, good or bad, about the Blessed Virgin, nor the order of Carmelites neither."

"Well, well," said Pat, "was there Carmelites nine hundred years before our Saviour was born, and were they Christians then ?"

"Why, the book makes it out they're that old," said Jem, "and that they took up with the Blessed Virgin as soon as she was born, and that she was mighty fond of them, and gave them the Scapular herself. But, 'deed she was in no hurry to give it to them, for she didn't give it them for more nor *twelve hundred years* after that again !"

"And how could that be, at all, at all ?" said Pat ; "sure she must have been dead before that anyway."

"Why, here's the story," said Jem (page 31). "There was one Simon Stock, that lived in England—and a quare way he got his name, for he ran away into the woods when he was twelve years old—and he lived in a hollow tree for twenty years, and he lived on the roots he scraped up, only when a dog brought him bread in his mouth on the festival days ; and the Blessed Virgin would be coming to him often : and it so fell out that was the time that the Carmelites was turned out of Mount Carmel. So the Blessed Virgin told him one day that they were coming that way, and that he'd be a Carmelite ; and so, when they come, he joined them, and was the greatest man that ever they had."

"Well, and did she give him the Scapular then ?" said Pat.

"Not that time," said Jem; "but when he was near dying, and thinking what would the Carmelites do without him, he went to the Blessed Virgin, and told her all about it, and how all the Popes had confirmed the order, and all that they had done for it (p. 33). And so one day she come to him, just dressed the way she would be in heaven, and thousands of angels with her, and the Scapular ready in her hand ; and she says to him—see, here's the very words in the book (p. 34)—' *Receive, most beloved son* (says she), *the Scapular of thy order, a sign of my confraternity, a privilege both to thee and to all Carmelites, in which he that dieth shall not suffer eternal fire ; behold the sign of salvation, a safeguard in danger, the covenant of peace and everlasting alliance.*' And then she just gives it into his hand, and was gone in a minute ; and see, here's the very day, and it marked, the 16th of July, 1251."

"Well, I wonder did all that happen," says Pat.

"Well, I'm thinking," said Jem, "if the Blessed Virgin was so fond of the Carmelites for 1250 years before, and if the Scapular was so good for them, would she never give it to them before ? Why wouldn't she give it to them when she was visiting them so often on Mount Carmel, at the time when our Blessed Saviour was born ? Why would she leave them without it so long, and they so fond of her, and she so fond of them ?"

"There's reason in that, any way," said Pat; "and howsomever it isn't the ould religion. Why, sure, the Scapular isn't more nor six hundred years old yet, even by the book's story; and don't the Catholics cry out on the Protestants, because everything in their religion isn't as old as the apostles ?"

"Well," said Jem, "I think there's a better way still to see if the story is true."

"And how's that?" said Pat.

"Why," said Jem, "just to see how we are to be saved by the Scapular, and how that fits with our being saved by Jesus Christ, the way the Bible tells us; for if the two doesn't fit, it's reason that only one of them can be true."

"Well, I'll stand to that," said Pat; "and how does the book say the Scapular saves us ?"

"Why, first of all," said Jem, "the book says it is a grand thing for people to be joined in societies, because then every one in the society gets a share in all the prayers, and sacrifices, fastings, alms, and mortifications, and of all the good works of all the rest."—Preface, p. 1.

And then Pat scratched his head for a minute, and, said he, "And who's the gainer by that, I wonder, or who's the loser? Why, there won't be more good works among them after all; and how will they divide? If every man gets his own (and that's the fairest) I don't see the gain at all. And if they get share and share alike, why them that does the most is the losers; and them that does nothing is the gainers. Sure enough there was short commons here in the famine; but if every one, big and little, in the parish, had brought all they had together to eat it at wonst, sure it wouldn't go farther? And if all the boys in the parish was working at task-work, and all in under one, to divide all the earnings among them, I'm thinking maybe its less work would be done, for all the lazy fellows would be saving themselves, to get their share of the wages, and they doing nothing. So I don't see the good of clubbing all together, no ways."

"Well, that's like enough, Pat," said Jem; "I don't see no great good in it so far; but, then, there's more in it still: sure the book says that

Pope Clement VII. has given the Scapularians a share of all the pious actions which are done throughout the whole church of God (page 46), and wouldn't that be making more for the Scapularians anyway ?"

"And, mercy on us," said Pat, "what right has the Pope to take their good works off them that does them, to give them all to the Scapularians ? Why, if I'd stint the children, to give the bit to a poor creature on the road, for the love of God, what right has the Pope to take that off me, to give it to them that never done it ? Sure I'm not the fool to think the Pope can do that, or that God Almighty will let him handle us that sort."

"Nor I neither, Pat," said Jem, "for doesn't the Bible say that every man 'must appear before the judgment seat of Christ ; that every man may receive the things done in his body, according to that HE *hath done*, whether it be good or bad' (2 Cor. v. 10) ? and, sure, how can the Pope go again that ?"

"Well, now," said Pat, "I mind a story I was reading in St. Matthew's Gospel, a Sunday, and there was ten virgins that was going out to meet the Bridegroom (and that was the Lord himself), and they had to fetch lamps with them, for belike it was night, and there was five of them had no oil for their lamps, and, the creatures, they just wanted to have all in common ; but the wise ones wouldn't agree to that at all, for they said they hadn't enough to be doing that with ; so them that had no oil didn't get in at all, and Jesus Christ said that's just the way it would be when he'd be coming in glory ; so it's plain that what's borrowed won't stand then ; and isn't that enough for that ?"

"Well, I think it is, Pat," said Jem, "and so we'll go on a bit, for there's more in it yet. Sure here's a chapter to say that them that dies in the Scapular will never suffer hell fire ; and the quare proof the book gives of it too ; for see what it says here (p. 48)—'In the city of Quarena, during the procession of the Holy Scapular, which is made on the third Sunday of every month, the devils were heard to execrate the Holy Scapular with many howlings and outcries, lamenting them-selves that, by means of this sacred habit of the Blessed Virgin, the gates of hell were shut to many persons.'"

"And does it mean that them that dies with the Scapular on will never go to hell if they were ever so bad ?" said Pat.

" Well, them's the words that the book says the Blessed Virgin spoke to Simon Stock, 'in which he that dieth shall not suffer eternal fire'" (p. 34), said Jem ; "but still the book won't stand to it all out : for it says, it only means that if any one that dies with the Scapular on does go to hell it will be his own fault, because God did enough for him" (pp. 48 and 49).

"Well, and wasn't that true for 1250 years before there was a Scapular at all?" said Pat, "and isn't it true now to them that never saw a Scapular?   But I doubt poor Judy doesn't take it that way."

"Well," said Jem, "here's a whole chapter about what Judy said, 'that the Blessed Virgin would go down to Purgatory, to take out the Scapularians the very next Saturday after they die.'   And, well, it turns out that that isn't in what the Blessed Virgin said to Simon Stock at all ; but it was the Popes done that ; and here the book gives us a list of five Popes, no less, that all laid it on the Blessed Virgin to do that same (p. 50) ; and what do you think of that, Pat ?"

"Why, then, Jem," said Pat, " I'd think it a great pity that ever they'd die at all, barring of a Friday night."

"Well, Pat," said Jem, "here's more ; here's a whole chapter of all the indulgences that ever the Popes gave to the Carmelites, for the foolishest things that ever you read. Sure here's an indulgence of three years to all Christians, let alone Carmelites, for every time they call the Carmelites 'the order of the Blessed Virgin Mary' (p. 55). Now, isn't that easy got ?"

"Well, salvation's cheap by the Scapular, anyway," said Pat.

"I'm thinking it's not, Pat," said Jem ; "for if the Bible's true, the Scapular will, maybe, cost their souls to them that trusts in it."

"And is there any more in it ?" said Pat.

''Deed is there," said Jem ; "sure here's a whole chapter, to show that the Scapular is good against 'devils, and fire, and water, and wild beasts, and sickness, aud witchcrafts, and danger in child-bed, and pistol-shots, and many other ill accidents' (p. 71) ; and here's stories for them all: first and foremost, here's a story of a man that was shot with a pistol and two bullets in it, and the minute he was shot he just felt the two bullets fall down into his breeches ; and when he got home, he found they just hit on the Scapular" (p. 69).

"Stop a bit, Jem," said Pat, "wouldn't that be the fine thing for Mr. Collins, the agent, that's shot at so often? I'm thinking, if that was true, he'd be a Scapularian himself."

"That would be the thing for the agents, Pat," said Jem; "but here's more stories for you: here's a poor fellow that was kept alive by the Scapular for four hours after the whole heart was shot out of him by a cannon ball; and sure it was the pity that he died at all—and here's a man got out of the sea by it, and here's a great fire put out by it."

"Well, that won't do anyway," said Pat: "didn't I know Peter Brady, that took his family off to America, and weren't they all Scapularians, and didn't the ship take fire before they got out of Liverpool, and wasn't there both fire and water there to try the Scapular on, and weren't they all drowned?"

"I mind that well, too, Pat," said Jem, "and sure enough it did them little good, the creatures."

"But what have the Scapularians to do for all this?" said Pat.

"Why, just not one haporth, but only to wear the Scapular on their backs, for it won't do no good at all if it's worn on the breast (p. 59) ; sure here it is, ' It sufficeth that the Scapular be received lawfully, and worn devoutly, without any other obligation ' (p. 60) ; only, if they want to get out of Purgatory on the first Saturday, they must fast on Wednesdays, or else say the Office of the Blessed Virgin, which they please ; but they must do neither the one nor the other to be kept out of hell."

"Well, isn't it the poor thing that creatures like Judy should be striving to get salvation by the Scapular, and not knowing or thinking about the blood of Jesus Christ ?" said Pat ; " and isn't it the poor thing that the clergy has never one word to say agin books like that, but if a Bible turns up afore them, they're ready to hunt it like a mad dog ? Surely there's something wanting to set it right."

" And with all, Pat," said Jem, " there's something in the Scapular itself that won't fit Father John."

" And what's that, Jem ?" said Pat.

" Here it is, Pat," said Jem : " ' Those that visit our churches (that's the Carmelite churches), and pray for the ordinary necessities, may free a soul out of Purgatory every Wednesday throughout the whole year' (p. 57) ; and where's the use in buying Masses if that's true?"

"Well," said Pat, "if the people once come to take that plan, isn't it Father John that will hunt the Scapular out of the parish ?"

"It might be better nor hunting the readers," said Jem.

So Pat and Jem parted for that night.

CHAPTER XIV.

PAYING THE DEBT.

"WELL, Pat, how is it with you now ?" said Jem, when they next met on the road.

"I don't know, Jem," said Pat ; "I'm down entirely."

"And what are you down for at all ?" said Jem : "has Father John been at you agen?"

"No, Jem, it's not that," said Pat ; "it's worse entirely."

"And what's the matter at all ?" said Jem.

"Why, it's afeard I am that the Bible's setting me astray after all," said Pat.

"And what's the matter at all with the Bible ?" said Jem.

"Why, it's troubling my mind in me," said

Pat. "Sure, before I read the Bible, my mind was uneasy enough, not knowing nothing at all ; and didn't I think, when I'd know the Bible, I'd have no trouble at all ? and now my mind is more troubled in me nor ever, and I can't get it quiet at all."

"And what is it that's troubling it at all ?" said Jem.

"Why, then, it's showing me how wicked I am," said Pat ; "and it's showing me how good I ought to be, and how I ought to love God entirely, and do everything in life for the love of God ; and, then, it's so hard to love God entirely, and it seems as if my heart couldn't love Him at all ; and it's telling me to love my enemies, and Father John itself, and it's so hard to do that anyway. But it's the badness of my heart entirely that the Bible's showing me ; and what will become of me at all if it's so bad ? And, then, evermore it's coming into my mind that the Bible is setting me astray."

"Well, Pat," says Jem, "sure you're not that bad ; sure you're not worse nor another ; sure all the neighbours calls you a decent, quiet, civil boy, and sure you're taken to reading the Bible."

"Well, but it isn't what the neighbours says

of me," said Pat; "what does that signify? Isn't it what God says of me, when He looks just straight into my heart? It's that that signifies; and don't I feel entirely that I'm a sinner, and nothing but a sinner? And doesn't the Bible itself say—'The soul that sinneth, the same shall die'?—Ezekiel xviii. 4. And isn't that me? And doesn't it say—'The wicked shall be turned into hell'? and don't the Bible show me that I'm wicked; and what will I do at all, at all?"

"Well, Pat," said Jem, "if the Bible isn't agreeing with you, maybe, if you just put it away for a while, you could come back on it again, when it wouldn't trouble you so much."

"No, Jem," said Pat, "I can't do that at all. It's taken hold of me, and I can't get shut of it at all; and I wouldn't neither, Jem, for all it's done to me: what would I take to at all? Is it the Scapular, or the like of that, I'd take to? Or would I take to Father John and his cursing? And sure I can't do without something now. And what can I take to only the Bible? And I'll stick to that, if it kills me; sure *I know* nothing else can do me any good."

"Well, Pat," said Jem, "I'm sure the Bible's

good, too ; but why would it trouble you that way, when it doesn't set me astray ? "

" And isn't it as bad for you as for me, Jem ? " said Pat : "doesn't it make us all out to be as bad as other ? Doesn't it say, that ' *They are all under sin*,' and that every mouth is stopped (Rom. iii. 9, 19) ? and what *will* we do if not one of us at all can have one word to say at the great judgment of God ? "

" Well, Pat," said Jem, " I didn't think of it rightly before, and I don't know what we'll say at all ; only this, if we're all that bad, and all sinners entirely, doesn't God mean to save some of us any way, by Jesus Christ ? Sure you're not going to say, that there won't be none at all saved by Jesus Christ ? and if we're all sinners, sure some of us sinners will be saved by Christ."

" Well, Jem," said Pat, " that's the only thing that stands to me at all ; but, somehow, I don't see how that can be, and that's just what I want to come at."

" I'll tell you how we'll get it," said Jem : " won't we just go down to Mr. Owens, and ask him ? "

" Well, I'll try that any way," said Pat ; " for if any one can show it to us, he will."

So off they went to Mr. Owens. And when they got into his study, he asked them was there anything they wanted to talk about. So Pat let it all out then, and, said he, "Your reverence, the Bible's setting me astray entirely."

"And how is that?" said Mr. Owens.

"Why, your reverence," said Pat, "it's telling me that I'm a sinner entirely, and that all sinners will be turned into hell, and what will I do at all?"

"Well, that's all right, so far," said Mr. Owens: "if the Bible didn't tell you that, it would do you no good at all."

"And how's that, your reverence?" said Pat, for he thought it mighty odd.

"Did you know Jemmy Gougerty?" said Mr. Owens.

"Aye did I," said Pat; "didn't he die in the fever that came after the praties failed?"

"And what about him?" said Mr. Owens.

"Why, he just went raging mad with the fever," said Pat, "and he said he was quite well, better nor ever he was in his life, and that he didn't want a doctor at all."

"And didn't they send for the doctor?" said Mr. Owens.

"No, indeed," said Pat; "for his wife was dead, the creature, and there was none but the childer with him; and when he said he was quite well, they never thought the doctor was wanting at all."

"And the doctor told me, two days after," said Mr. Owens, "that that was just the case he could have cured, only he never was sent for at all."

"And what has that to do with me and the Bible, your reverence?" said Pat.

"Why, just this," said Mr. Owens, "that a man ought to know when he is sick and wants the doctor. Are there not many people that are mad about their souls, and don't know that they want Jesus Christ, the great physician of souls, at all?"

"Well, that's me, sure enough, your reverence," said Pat. "I was mad that way long, long enough; and the more I wanted Jesus Christ, the more I didn't know that I wanted him."

"Well, that's just what I mean," said Mr. Owens. "If the Bible didn't make you feel that you are a sinner, and that you want a Saviour, it would just be doing you no good at all."

"Well, it's done that for me any way," said Pat. "But how will I be saved if I'm a sinner? That's just what I want to know."

"Do you know Mr. Nulty?" said Mr. Owens.

"Well, I do," said Pat, "and many's the day I worked for him, and a good man he is."

"Is he good to the beggars?" said Mr. Owens.

"Well, he's mighty hard to them that chooses to live by begging, and won't work at all," said Pat; "but he's the best man at all to them that works hard, and can't do it. Don't I know Pat Flaherty, that works harder than any man in the parish, and didn't his cow die on him, and he hadn't the rent, and wasn't he processed and decreed for it, and hadn't the gripper a hold of him, to take him off to jail; and didn't Mr. Nulty come for'ad in the court, and just lay down the money for him?"

"And did the gripper take him to jail then?" said Mr. Owens.

"How could he," said Pat, "when the debt was paid for him?"

"Well, and if Jesus Christ should pay for your sins," said Mr. Owens, "what have you to fear from the gripper of souls?"

"Aye, and is that the way, your reverence?"

said Pat. "Well, I'm seeing it now, sure enough."

"Don't read *half* the Bible, Pat," said Mr. Owens; "that's a bad way—read it all; and if it makes you see that you are a sinner, and that you want a Saviour, it will make you see, too, that you have a Saviour, that is able and willing to save you. Just listen to this," said Mr. Owens (and he turned to 1 Tim. i. 15, Douay Bible, and read)—"A faithful saying, and worthy of all acceptation, that Christ Jesus came into the world to save sinners, of whom I am chief."

"And who was that, that was chief of sinners?" said Pat.

"It was the great Apostle St. Paul himself, that said that of himself," said Mr. Owens.

"And was he a great sinner?" said Pat.

"He calls himself 'chief of sinners,'" said Mr. Owens; "and look what he says here," said Mr. Owens, and he turned to Acts xxvi. 10, 11 —"Many of the saints did I shut up in prison . . . . and I punished them often in every synagogue, *and compelled them to blaspheme.*"

"And why did Jesus Christ take him for an apostle if he was that wicked?" said Jem.

"Read the next verse to what we read in the

Epistle to Timothy," said Mr. Owens; and he handed the book to Jem (and a Douay Bible it was). So Jem read—"But for this cause have I obtained mercy, that in me first Christ Jesus might show forth all patience, for the information of them that shall believe in him unto life everlasting."

" Well," said Pat, " that's good, for there's a pattern that he will save sinners."

" Listen to this," said Mr. Owens, and he read, from the Gospel of St. John iii. 16, the words of Christ himself—"God so loved the world as to give his only begotten Son, that *whosoever* believeth in him may not perish, but may have life everlasting." And then Mr. Owens went on—"Does not this show you that whatever is wanting to bring you to life everlasting, Jesus Christ is willing to do for you ?"

" It does, your reverence, and I'd like to know what he *will* do," said Pat.

" If you believe and trust in him," said Mr. Owens, "he will stand up for you at *the great day*, and say—'I have taken this man's sins upon myself, I have paid for all his sins, and his soul is mine, that I may save it for ever ;' and won't that do ?" said Mr. Owens.

"That's just what I want, your reverence, to make me happy," said Pat.

"Well," said Mr. Owens, " you have read your Bible to some purpose, to see that you want a Saviour ; now read your Bible again, to see what that Saviour did for you, and you will find comfort for your soul."

So Pat went home with a hopeful mind that night, and we hope to hear more of his reading yet.

CHAPTER XV.

THE SERMON.

" WELL, Pat, what were you doing since I saw you ?" said Jem, when they met next.

" Well, then, I was hearing a sermon in Kilcommon," said Pat.

" And was it Father John that was in it ?" said Jem.

" No, then," said Pat, " it was Doctor Martin, from England, that was a Protestant clergyman, and that turned ; and I saw it up in letters as big as my hand, so I thought I'd go and see if he came up to Father John."

" Well, and how did he do it ?" said Jem. ·

" Well, he's a great preacher entirely," said Pat, " and no mistake, for you would hear him a mile off. But for what he said, it beat all that ever I heard from ourselves itself. Why, sure he spoke it out plain, that the Blessed Virgin was the wife of the Holy Ghost !* Now, is that in the Bible, I want to know ?"

* Pat is, probably, correct in this, shocking as it may appear, for we find a similar statement in a report of a sermon, preached at Navan, by Dr. Marshall, in 1852; published by T. Henderson, Kells.

"Why, Pat," said Jem, "sure that beats ourselves all out; sure that's worse nor ever we were. Doesn't the Blessed Virgin call herself the handmaid of the Lord? And to go to make a woman the wife of God! sure that beats all. And didn't God say that man and wife are one flesh? and how can she be one flesh with Him? Sure it's too bad entirely."

"And how comes it at all," said Pat, "that the great English clergy, that has learning and knowledge, should be turning to worse than the likes of us can stand?"

"Well, I heard Mr. Owens preach a sermon on that," said Jem, "and he made it plain enough, for he said our hearts was all turned away from the truth by nature, and that the wise and learned was as bad this way as the poorest creatures; and he showed that it wasn't the wise and learned that was mostly called,* but that the Gospel was preached to the poor,† and that God had chosen the foolish to confound the wise;‡ and if that was the way in St. Paul's own time, why wouldn't it be that way now? And he said, foreby, that the most learned of those clergy that

* 1 Cor. i. 26.　　　† Matt. xi. 5; Luke iv. 18.
‡ 1 Cor. i. 27.

turned in England didn't give any learned reason for it at all; but just no better nor ourselves would give, when the priest told us that his way was right ;* and sure that's the poor proof, when it isn't in the Bible. And isn't it enough to make out Mr. Owens right, when Dr. Martin says the like of that ? But what more did he say ?"

"Well, of all that ever you heard he said of the Protestant clergy. He said he knew them well, for he was one himself; and that they didn't believe in God, or in Jesus Christ, or in the Holy Ghost itself; but that they was all infidels and heathens."

"Well, it'll go hard with me before I take his word that Mr. Owens does not believe in God or in Jesus Christ," said Jem ; "but what more, Pat ?"

"Well, he said that they didn't care about the souls of the people at all, and that, with all the talk they made, they didn't want the people to turn Protestants at all, but only to pretend to do it ; and that they gave the people five pounds apiece only just to pretend it ; and him getting

* See the CATHOLIC LAYMAN for March, 1852, vol. I., page 23.

five pounds for preaching that same sermon, as I heard tell."

"Well, stop there a bit, Pat," said Jem; "if the priest thought that the five pounds apiece was really going, would he give it out in the chapel that way? Doesn't he know there would be plenty to look for it, if it was to be got? And, if it was true, wouldn't he be more likely to tell the people they wouldn't get the money at all, and they needn't go to look for it?"

"Well, signs by," said Pat, "I was up with Mr. Owens next day, and who should I see at the door but Molly Brady; and Mr. Owens comes out and asks her what she wants: 'Your reverence,' says she, 'I'm a girl that wants to turn;' and so Mr. Owens began to talk to her about the reasons for turning: and Molly kept looking at him mighty hard; and at last says she, 'But what are yees goin' to give me?' says she. 'So,' says Mr. Owens, 'we're going to give you the Word of God,' says he, 'that's able to save your soul.' 'And won't yees give me the five pounds?' says she. So when he told her that was all a lie, she went off in a huff; so I overtook her goin' back, 'and who told you that, Molly?' says I. 'Father John did,' says she.

' And will you believe Father John again ?' says I. ' Why would I,' says she, ' when he made that fool of me ? and wasn't I the fool to believe him at all ?' says she; ' sure I might have knowd,' says she, ' that he never told one word of truth in his life, barrin' he mistook it for a lie,' says she."

" Ay," said Jem, " and didn't I hear of ould Judy Callaghan, a while back, when Father John gave it out in the chapel that Mr. Owens would give a leg of mutton and a blanket to every woman in the parish that would turn. And up goes Judy to Mr. Owens next day ; and, ' Your reverence,' says she, ' I'm come to give myself up to you, for the leg of mutton and the blanket.' ' And, my poor woman,' says he, ' is it possible you would sell your soul and your religion for a leg of mutton ?' ' Oh ! no, your reverence,' says she, ' oh ! no, dear, not without the blanket.' "

" Well, Jem," said Pat, " I'm of your notion, that if the priests believed it themselves they'd deny it in the chapel, in place of giving it out ; but where's the use of talking ? don't we know it's not true at all ; and don't we know that what Mr. Owens wants is to get us to read the Bible, and to live by it ?"

"Well, we know that, any way," said Jem; "but if it's all true what the Bible says of tellin' lies, what will be done with all the lies that's told in the chapel?"

"Well, it's hard to expect truth from them that tells lies," said Pat; "and I mind I read a speech in the newspaper, a while back, that said, the worst thing at all in the Irish was, that they mostly tell lies entirely, and won't tell a word of truth, if they can help it; and sure that's not far off the real thing."

"Ay," said Jem, "I thought that the other day, when I was at the fair of Ballybrack; and there was young Mr. Williams selling a horse, and he had old Peter M'Kenna with him, that sells for all the gentlemen; and there comes up a man and asks about the horse; and Mr. Williams just answers him fairly; and if you had seen how old Peter scoulded him afterwards. 'What made you go tell him the truth at all?' says he. 'Why, sure what I said did the horse no harm,' says Mr. Williams. 'And what do I care for harm or no harm?' says Peter; 'while you're a living man,' says he, 'never go for to tell one word of truth upon a street.' And, thinks I to myself, it's the rule of the street, sure enough, and it's liars we are entirely."

"And what else would we be," said Pat, "when we know nothing at all of what God says of the judgment on liars ; and when we see the priest tell lies himself at the altar of God ? Sure is there a man in the chapel that knows what God says, that all liars shall have their part in the lake that burns with fire and brimstone ? And is not that enough to show that the people ought to have the Bible, to know what God says, and what God will do ?"

Who knows but that Pat and Jem, and many a poor man like them, may help to bring the Irish people to a knowledge of these things?

CHAPTER XVI.

THE STATION.

"WELL, Pat, what have you got to talk of this time?" said Jem.

"The STATION, Jem," said Pat.

"And is it at a station you were, Pat?" said Jem.

"'Deed is it, Jem," said Pat "without meaning a bit of it."

"And how did you get there at all without meaning it, Pat?" said Jem.

"Why, I was going by Pat Devine's public-house," said Pat, "and there was a deal of people about it, but I didn't know what was going on, and I just went in for a pen'orth of baccy, and there I was in it, afore I knew where it was; and then, sure enough, I seen it was Father John holding a station in the inner room; and when I got the baccy, I was making my lucky, when I heard Molly Devine, and Mary Gormly, and Sal Gougerty, and some more of the devotest women, that's always at their duties, bragging again each other what was the best thing in the Church of Rome to trust in for our salvation, and then I just stopped a bit, to hear what they would say."

"Well, I suppose they were all of the one mind, anyway," said Jem.

"Not a bit of it, Jem," said Pat; "there was no two of them of the one way of thinking; just one thing better than another, taking their pick and choice like; and, 'deed, there seemed to be a something for every one, no matter how many."

- "Well, the more hope some one hit right," said Jem.

Tim Tevlin's cheap absolution.   Discussion as to the relative merits of Holy Water, Holy Oil, the Mass, and the Scapular.

"I'm afeard not, Jem," said Pat, "for there was one thing nobody took hold to."

"And what did they take hold on, Pat ?" said Jem.

"Why, Molly Devine allowed it was the Mass, 'for sure,' says she, 'that's best of all ; isn't it offering the body and blood, and soul and divinity, for the living and the dead ?' says she. And then Mary Gormly allowed it was the holy water ; 'for sure when I have plenty of that by me,' says she, 'I don't care for charms, nor fairies, nor the devil himself,' says she ; 'and what need I want anything clse,' says she, 'when I don't care for the devil itself, with the holy water on me ?'   And then Sal Gougerty allowed it was the Scapular, 'for sure that'll get me to heaven the next Saturday after I die,' says she, 'and what need I want of anything else ?' says she.   And old Peggy Donohue says, 'Sure it's confession,' says she, 'for when the priest says the Latin over me, won't I be as clean of sin as the child unborn,' says she, 'and what more do I want than that,' says she, 'and what are yees all here for with your shillings, if that's not the thing ?' says she.   And then old Nancy Smith just riz on them all. 'And sure,' says she, 'it's

astray yees are entirely ; sure isn't one drop of
the holy oil worth them all ?' says she : ' if I get
one drop of that on me before the breath is out
of me, what need I care for anything else ?' says
she.   And now do you see, Jem, what none of
them thought of to trust in ?"

"Ay do I," said Jem.   "Sure none of them
knows that it's in their own Bible that *the blood
of Jesus Christ his Son cleanseth from all sin.*
And isn't it the poor thing that none of them
thinks of trusting in that, the creatures ? and
isn't it the quare thing, if they are all Catholics,
that they don't all trust in the *same thing*, but
one taking one thing, and another another thing?
but sure that's the way with them.   But, Pat,
now did you tell them of the blood of Christ, and
you at a station ?"

"Well, 'deed then I did, Jem," said Pat.
"Says I, girls, isn't the blood of Christ the
best thing at all, for sure that cleanses from all
sin ?"

"And how did they take that at all, Pat ?"
said Jem.

"Well, Jem," said Pat, "they just darned
their eyes in me, as if they never heard the like
of that before ; but I hadn't time to hear more of

it, for Pat Daly was just coming out of the room where Father John was hearing confessions, and he just got hearing what I said, so he turned round on me, and, ' Is it a Souper you are, to bring the like of that to a station with you ?' says he. ' Not a bit of it,' says I ; ' I takes no soup, thank God,' says I. And that's true, any-way, for not a drop of soup crossed my carcase since the Relief Committee gave it out in the famine. And I just turned round again on him, and, says I—' Are you going to tell us that the Soupers will have the blood of Christ all to themselves, and the Catholics get none of it ?' says I ; and with that he just quit it. Well, who do you think I seen go in next, Jem ?"

" I don't know, Pat," said Jem.

" Well, if it wasn't Tim Tevlin," said Pat.

" Is it him," said Jem, " the poacher and sheep stealer, that never did an honest day's work in his life, and a Ribbonman into the bar-gain ? What does the likes of him want of absolution ?"

" Well, now," said Pat, " if Father John can wipe out a man's sins with a turn of his hand, isn't that just the man for him to try on ?"

"Well, sure enough," said Jem; "but did he get absolution?"

"Well, I'll tell you about that," said Pat, "for the door stood open a minute, and I just seen it. There was the wee table, you know, with the plate on to drop the shilling in, just forenint the door, and Tim was giving it the go by. 'Where's the shilling?' says Father John. 'Haven't got it, your reverence,' says Tim. 'Go off with you and get it,' says Father John. 'And where will I get it, your reverence?' says Tim. 'What's that to me?' says Father John: 'off with you and get it.' And so Tim stood there quite easy. 'What are you waiting for there?' says Father John. 'Won't your reverence give me absolution?' says Tim. 'You'll get none without the shilling; be off out of that for it,' says Father John. So Tim stood there as easy as you please. 'What are you standing there for?' says Father John. 'Will I steal it, your reverence?' says Tim. 'Be off for the shilling, and don't bother me,' says Father John, with a screech. Well, Tim seen Father John was minding nothing, he was that mad, and Tim had got just foreninst the table, and, as he was turning round, he just drops his hand in the plate, and lifts the shilling, and walks out, and away out of the house. And, a while after, in comes Tim; and when the next man comes out, in goes Tim. 'And have you the shilling now?' says Father John. 'Yes, your reverence,' says Tim, dropping the shilling in the plate; 'but sure I had to steal it, your reverence,' says he. Well, you never seen a man so deaf as Father John. He never heard a word, but just says—'Down on your knees,' says he. And then the door shut to, and I seen no more till Tim comes out, looking as pleased as if he had stole the best sheep in a flock."

"Well, now, I wonder," said Jem, "would the absolution do for stealing the shilling?"

"And why wouldn't it," said Pat: "didn't he confess it, and get absolution?"

"Well, maybe it was as good for that as for all the rest," said Jem; "but did you go in yourself, Pat?"

"No, indeed, then, I didn't," said Pat, "but I was mighty 'feard Father John would have caught me, and lugged me in, maybe; for, a while after, out comes Father John in a hurry, and, 'Boys,' says he, 'is that Pat Doyle going down the street?' 'It is, your reverence,' says severals. 'Out with you, boys, and fetch him in to me,' says Father John. So off the boys went. Well, you know, Jem, Pat Doyle is taken up with the Readers, and has quit the Mass altogether, and goes to Church; so in he comes with the boys; and 'deed it's the dark corner I got into then; and then Father John says to Pat Doyle, 'Are you come to confession?' says he. 'No,' your reverence,' says Pat Doyle; 'I confessed my sins to God this morning.' 'Much good that'll do you,' says Father John; 'what were you promised for turning?' says he. So Pat Doyle didn't say a word. 'Was it money?' says Father John; 'was it five pounds?' 'No, your reverence,' says Pat Doyle. 'Was it meal,' says Father John. 'No, your reverence,' says Pat Doyle. 'Was it soup?' says Father John. 'No, your reverence,' says Pat Doyle. 'And what was it you were promised?' says Father John; 'tell it out, man, before the people,' says he. 'Salvation, your reverence,' says Pat Doyle. Well, Father John looked done for a minute anyway; and then, says he, 'Are you coming back to Mass?' says he. 'No, your reverence,' says Pat Doyle. 'And what will you and your children live on if you don't, when you were promised nothing?' says Father John. 'Please, your reverence,' says Pat Doyle, 'we'll live on the blossoms of the bushes afore we go back.' Well, if I wasn't thinking what would come on Pat Doyle, or myself too, if I was caught, when who should come in but the Rev. Mr. Owens himself; for he was coming up the street, and he seen Pat Doyle fetched in to the station, and just followed him in, and he just comes right up to Father John, and says to him, 'Sir, it was I that took this man, Pat Doyle, away from your Mass, for I showed him that the sacrifice of Christ was finished on the cross, never more to be repeated; and that no Christian man should bow down in worship to a wafer. And I am ready now, sir, to show you, before the people, why no Christian man should do so, if you will undertake to show them why they should.' 'Pat Devine! where's Pat Devine?' says Father John. 'Here, sir,' says Pat. 'Is it getting my horse you are? Will he never be ready?' says Father John. 'Yes, sir: coming, sir,' says Pat Devine, and out he comes with the horse in a hurry. 'Oh, your reverence,' says Peggy Donoghue, 'sure you won't go without hearing

my confession?'   'Oh! your reverence,' says
Sal Gougerty, and all of them, 'won't you stop
a bit for us?'   'Out of the way, women,' says
Father John; 'is it all day I'll be kept here?'
And up he gets on his horse, with Pat Devine
holding the bridle and the stirrup, and flattering
him all he could, and I peeping out of the open
window: and I seen, as he rode off, that Pat
Devine just turned the wrong side of his hand
after him; and says he, 'The back of my hand
to you, that wouldn't stand up for your Church
and your religion.'"

"Well, Pat," said Jem, "sure Paddy Doyle
puts us all to shame, that wasn't afeard to stand
up like a man."

"Well, maybe so," said Pat; "but sure why
can't a man keep it all to himself, when it sets
the country against him? Sure I trust in nothing
but Christ and His blood, that cleanseth from all
sin : but why would I go to say that out, and
bring trouble on myself?"

Who knows but the time is coming when Pat
himself will say it before men? Pat does not
know it, nor mean it now. But the time comes
to every one that truly trusts in Christ, when

something in their breasts within will *make* them confess Christ before men ; for otherwise Christ would have to deny them before His Father in heaven.*

CHAPTER XVII.

THE POTATO-ROT.

WELL, Pat and Jem were digging Mr. Nulty's potatoes, and it was a sorrowful sight to see, for half the potatoes, and more, were bad ; and every one looked sad and sorry, and the poor fellows had hardly the heart to dig. And Pat and Jem had two ridges next each other ; and they talked a little betimes.

" Well, Jem," said Pat, " it's not like praty-digging in old times, when praty-digging was pleasant ; when every man seen his work just done for that year, and enough before him for the winter."

" Aye, Pat," said Jem, " and a bit of a fire at the rig's end, with the childer roasting the praties in the ashes ; but I doubt we will never see that again."

* See St. Matthew's Gospel, x. 33 ; and St. Mark, viii. 38.

"I wonder how it came at all, or what came on the praties at all, at all," said Pat.   "Sure there was praties long enough, and never no disease in them ; I wonder *how* it come at all."

"One thing's plain enough, Pat," said Jem, "it was God done it Himself, or let it be done, surely ; but still I'm wondering *why* He let it come upon poor creatures ?"

"I wonder would the Bible tell us anything about it," said Pat ; "I mind now reading about famines, and the Bible allowed it was God sent them, and I'm thinking it allowed, too, it was for the wickedness of the country He sent them."

"Well, sure, that's like enough," said Jem, "and we'll have a look for that same when the work's done."

Well, they could not talk a great deal, because they were so busy ; but they had a word now and again.   And, when they were going home,

"I wonder," said Pat, "what Father John makes it out to be for ?"

"Well, I'll tell you that," said Jem, "for a man that was in chapel on Sunday told me ; he said Father John allowed it was the readers done it ; for that the readers was come out of the towns of Sodom and Gomorra, in England, that is the wickedest places at all; and that people coming out of them towns here is enough to bring down the vengeance of God upon Ireland entirely; and it was that done it all on the praties, by Father John's account; and, 'deed, as I heard, he said enough to make the people put the readers out of Ireland entirely, and out of the world, too, if they only believed the half what Father John told them."

"And I wonder," said Pat, "does Father John think that Sodom and Gomorra is in England? Don't I know them places is in the Bible, and not in England? But it's little Father John minds what he says, when he thinks the people knows nothing about it. But how did the praty disease come seven or eight years ago, when there was no readers here at all, and no one thinking about the Bible? Sure, didn't all the stir about the Bible begin after the praties got bad? and how would the readers bring it afore they came themselves?"

"Well, I'm thinking," said Jem, "Father John's reason is as bad as his cure; sure, didn't Mr. Smith get a mass said for his praties one time, and it's little the better they were of it; and didn't I go to Father John the first year myself, like the fool I was then, and didn't he give me holy water to put rouud the heaps for a cure, and didn't every praty in it turn bad on me? and why would his reason be better thau his cure ?"

"Aye, and don't I mind the second year," said Pat, "when all the country was going to the Blessed Priest* up in Tullybricken, that was put out of his parish by the bishop for bad living, for blessed salt to put on their praties at setting time (and the nice little living he made for himself out of the poor creatures with his blessed salt), and didn't they all turn out one worse nor another? and after that it's little I mind what the priests say about the praty rot. Sure, it's plain enough that the Lord doesn't let on to them what He is going to do, and why would we look to them for the reason of it ?"

"Well, Pat," said Jem, "I'm thinking if any reason is to be got for it all, it's in the Bible we will get it. And, sure, don't we know that

---

* Our readers may have observed that, in Ireland, a Blessed Priest—that is, a priest who pretends to the power of working miracles—is almost always one who has been put out of his parish for immoral conduct ; perhaps because he has no other way of living, and such a one has no scruple at living by lies. But these Blessed Priests are much fewer in the country than they used to be ; perhaps because the people are getting more sense.

nothing but God's own Word can tell beforehand what He is going to do, or the reason of anything that it pleases Him to do? and them that doesn't stick to his Word, nor doesn't want the people to see it, sure, it's not them we ought to look to to know what He does, or what He means."

Well, as they were walking along, they fell in with the Rev. Mr. Owens; and when they had bid the time of day, Mr. Owens asked what they were doing; and they said, digging Mr. Nulty's potatoes; so Mr. Owens asked how the potatoes turned out; and then, says Pat,

"Why, your reverence, the praties are bad entirely under every clod you turn up."

"Aye," said Mr. Owens; "did you never read anything like that in the Bible?"

"No, your reverence," said Jem; "but we were just wondering would it be there."

So Mr. Owens took out his Bible, and read, "Is not the meat cut off before our eyes, yea, joy and gladness from the house of our God: the seed is rotten under their clods."—Joel i. 16, 17.

"And, your reverence," said Jem, "will you

tell us *why* God does the like at all ; for sure it be to be Him that does it."

"That's true, certainly," said Mr. Owens ; "for the Scripture says, ' *The Lord hath called for a famine,* and it shall come on the land seven years.' "—2 Kings viii. 1. (4 Kings, Douay).

" And does the Bible tell us anything about the reason of it, your reverence ?" said Jem.

" Surely it does," says Mr. Owens ; "listen to this ;" so Mr. Owens read, " Shall there be evil in a city and the Lord hath not done it ?* Surely the Lord will do nothing but He revealeth His secret unto His servants the prophets."—Amos iii. 6, 7.

" Well, your reverence," said Pat, "that's just it ; we want to know the secret of it. Is it for the wickedness of the people that God does it all ?"

" That is the reason that God's Word gives," said Mr. Owens. " Listen to this—' Alas ! for all the evil abominations of the house of Israel ! for they shall fall by the sword, by the famine,

---

* " Which the Lord hath done ?" (Douay Bible). The meaning is that all judgment is from God. The note on this verse in the Douay Bible is a good one ; " He speaks of the evil of punishments of war, famine, pestilence, desolation, &c., but not of the evil of sin, of which God is not the authór."

and by the pestilence; . . . then shall ye know that I am the Lord.' "—Ezekiel vi. 11, 13.

"And what sort of sins is it for, your reverence?" said Pat.

"For all sins, and for all turning away from God," said Mr. Owens; "but there are some sins that are specially marked. In the next chapter we read—'Make a chain, for the land is full of bloody crimes' (ch. vii. 23); and in ch. xxxiii. 25—'Ye shed blood, and shall ye possess the land?'"

"Well," said Pat, "if it wasn't on the road, fornent that very field, that Mr. Browne, the agent, was shot about land, and the people all working in that very field, and·looking on, and not one of them would tell which way the men went that did it!"

"Yes," said Mr. Owens, "the people were banded together then to shed innocent blood for the possession of the land, and God has scattered them off the land since. That is a sin that cries to God against a land; and so does forgetting God, and turning away from the knowledge of his holy word and will."

"And does your reverence think it was all for the sins of the Catholics?" said Jem.

"Indeed, I do not, Jem," said Mr. Owens; "we have all had our sins and our forgetfulness of God and of his word, and his dealings are meant for us all."

"But, your reverence," said Pat, "there's one thing that puzzles me still. When God sent the curse on the praties didn't he hurt them that loved and served him, as well as them that turned away from him? and wouldn't that be enough to make them turn away from him too? Sure your reverence's praties were as bad as Father John's, every bit," said Pat, scratching his head.

"We never understand any of God's dealings rightly," said Mr. Owens, "until we learn to understand his love and goodness first. 'He doth not willingly afflict or grieve the children of men'—(Lamentations iii. 33). The prophet Joel, who spoke of the seed being rotten under the clods, has showed us that, even to the wicked, God's vengeance is sent in mercy. Just listen to this—'Therefore, also, now saith the Lord, turn ye even to me with all your heart, and with fasting, and with weeping, and with mourning; and rend your hearts and not your garments and turn unto the Lord your God; for He is gracious and merciful, slow to anger, and of

great kindness, and repenteth Him of the evil."
—(Joel ii. 12, 13.)   Did you ever read our
Saviour's parable of the Prodigal Son, in St.
Luke's Gospel?" said Mr. Owens, turning to Pat.

"I did, your reverence," said Pat.

"And what brought him back to his father?"
said Mr. Owens.

"It was the famine, your reverence; I mind
that well," said Pat.   (See St. Luke's Gospel,
xv. 14, &c.)

"And there has been a worse famine in Ireland than any we have been talking about," said
Mr. Owens; "a famine that makes souls perish;
'Not a famine of bread, nor a thirst for water,
but of hearing the words of the Lord.'—(Amos,
viii. 11.)   And don't you see, Pat, that since
God sent the disease on the potatoes, He is bringing the people to seek for the Word of God;
isn't that using the potato famine to drive out a
worse famine?"

"That's truth, your reverence," said Jem.

"And don't you be afraid," said Mr. Owens,
turning to Pat again, "that those that knew and
served God will turn away because He sends
them trials: if God means *judgment in mercy* to
them that forget Him, much more to them that

know Him : 'whom the Lord loveth he chas-
teneth," and He tells them that to comfort them
—(Hebrews xii. 6). And then they can say
with St. Paul 'who shall separate us from the
love of Christ? Shall tribulation, or distress, or
persecution, or FAMINE, or nakedness, or peril, or
sword? . . . In all these things, we are
more than conquerors through Him that loved
us.' "—Rom. viii. 35, 37.

So then they were come to where Mr. Owens
must leave them to go his way, and he was bidding them good night kindly ; and Pat stopped
him for a minute, saying—

"One thing more, your reverence ; is Sodom
and Gomorra in England ; for Father John
allows it is ?"

So Mr. Owens said, "St. Peter tells us that
the Sodom and Gomorra that God destroyed by
fire from heaven were meant 'for an example to
those that after should live ungodly' ; and so,
wherever there are ungodly men, there is the
spiritual Sodom. But if Father John meant
that wherever the Bible is read *there* is Sodom
and Gomorra, you may judge for yourselves of
that. But if Father John was wise, he would
not talk so much of Sodom and Gomorra being

in England ; for fear we should show him, out of the Douay Bible, that Babylon is in Rome."*

So Mr. Owens bid them good night again, and the boys went home for that night, talking by the road of Mr. Owens and Father John.

* If the reader will look at the preface to St. Peter's 1st Epistle in the Douay Bible, he will read this : "He wrote it at Rome, which figuratively he calls Babylon ; " alluding to ch. v., 13.

CHAPTER XVIII.

HARD PLACES IN SCRIPTURE.

" WELL, Jem, I have come at the place that says the Bible is hard to be understood," said Pat, one day as they met.

" Well, I was looking out for that," said Jem, " but I didn't know where to find it, though I heard tell it was in it."

" Well, here it is," said Pat ; and he opened his Douay Bible at 2 Peter, ch. iii., v. 16.

" Tell us, then, does it bid us not read it ?" said Jem, in a great hurry, for he was beginning to be afraid, after all.

" Well," said Pat, " wouldn't it be the quare thing to write a letter to a man, and to put at the end of the letter for to not read what was in it ?"

" Well, that would be out of the way, surely," said Jem ; " but does it tell the man it was writ to, to not show it to any one else ?"

" Not a word at all again' reading," said Pat, " that I can find ; it says, sure enough, that there's some things hard to be understood ; but it surely does *not* say that it's best not to read."

"Who was it written to at all?" said Jem; and he laid hold of the book to see, but he couldn't make it out, for the beginning of that Epistle only says—"To them that have obtained *equal* faith with us" (Douay Bible).

"Them must be great Christians, surely," said Jem; "would it be for the likes of us at all?"

"Try *your* book, Jem," said Pat; for they had got a way of putting the two books together. So Jem tried his book and found it this way—"To them that have obtained *like precious** faith with us."

"Well, that would fit us better, surely," said Jem; "but how will we know about it?"

"Well, I made out who it was written to," said Pat; "for see here, at the first verse of the third chapter, he says, 'this *second* Epistle I write to you.' Now, doesn't that lay down that he wrote one before to the same people, and wouldn't that be the first Epistle? and look here," said Pat, turning over to the beginning of the first Epistle, "see here: this one is written 'to the strangers dispersed through Pontus, Galatia, Cappadocia, Asia, and Bithynia.' And

---

* This is the exact meaning of the Greek word which the Apostle wrote—ισοτιμον.

sure I met Mr. Owens's schoolmaster, and I asked him what places them were, and he told me they were all great countries, every one as big as Ireland; so you see, Jem, this Epistle was written to plenty of people, and would he go for to tell them not to read what he wrote to them? And if he wrote it to such lots of people, would he tell them not to show it to any one else? And more nor that, he wrote it to the very servants themselves in all them countries; for look here (and Pat read the eighteenth verse of the second chapter, Ep. 1,)—'Servants, be subject to your masters, with all fear;' so you see yourself the letter was to the servants, too, as well as to their betters; and isn't that coming near to the likes of us?"

"Well, let us mind the place well, and see what we can make of it," said Jem; for he was taking heart again about the reading, at what Pat said. So they read, "And account the long-suffering of our Lord Salvation; as also our most dear brother Paul, according to the wisdom given him, hath written to you; as also in all his Epistles, speaking in them of these things; in which are certain things hard to be understood, which the unlearned and unstable wrest—as they do also the other Scriptures—to their own destruction; you, therefore, brethren, knowing these things before, take heed lest being led aside by the error of the unwise, you fall from your own steadfastness." (Ep. 2, ch. 3, verses 15, 16, 17.)

"Now," said Pat, "if we weren't to read the Bible, wouldn't that be the place to say it in?"

"Well, that's the place it would fit, if it was to be said at all," said Jem.

"Well, and it *isn't* said, but only to take heed," said Pat.

"Well, that's true any way," said Jem, "and thanks be to God for that much itself. But still, Pat, sure it's said that the unlearned wrests the hard places to their own destruction; and sure it's little learning the like of us has."

"Well, I'm turning that over in my mind everyway," said Pat, "and I'm thinking that's said just the same of the *easy* places."

"Show me that again, Pat," said Jem; and he read that part over again, "which the unlearned and unstable wrest, *as they do also* THE OTHER SCRIPTURES, to their own destruction."

"Well that's it anyway," said Jem; "if there's any good in it at all, it's just as bad against the easy places as the hard places,"

"Well now, Jem," said Pat, "what makes the priest read out the Gospel at mass in plain English? Didn't I hear it said, afore now, that the Church allows the easy places, that ignorant people *can't* wrest to their own destruction, to be read out to them in chapel, and only keeps away the hard places that they *might* wrest to their destruction for want of learning? Now, if the unlearned wrests the easy places to their destruction, just the same way as they do the hard places, why would the one be read to them, no more nor the other? Answer me that now."

"Well, sure enough, Pat, you're right," said Jem; "and if *that* reason needn't stop the one, why should it stop the other? But let us see what caution St. Peter puts on it." So they read the next verse—"You, therefore, brethren, knowing these things before, take heed lest being led aside by the error of the unwise, you fall from your own steadfastness."

"Now, it's my opinion," said Pat, "if Father John had been at the writing of that verse, he would just have put down in place of it, ' Since you see the danger, *don't read the Bible :*' but you see, yourself, that St. Peter, that they allow was the first Pope, didn't say that anyway."

"True for you there, Pat," said Jem; "but let

us try and make out what caution St. Peter did give us."

So they set to work at that ; and says Pat, " I wonder what he means by the 'error of the unwise.' Wouldn't he tell us somewhere what that was ?"

So they set to work to read over that chapter well, and at last Pat put his finger on verse 5, and, said he, "why, here's people that's '*wilfully ignorant*,' and would it be them ?"

"Well, them's the scoffers in verse 3," said Jem ; "and see here's what they say in verse 4 —'where is his promise or his coming ? for since the time that the Fathers slept, all things continue as they were from the beginning of the creation.'"

So they set to study that, and then Jem said, "Why them is people that would get up in the last days, and scoff at the promise of Christ's coming to judgment ; and here's the reason they have—everything is going on for long enough, just the way it does now, and why won't it go on for ever just the same?   Now, would that be ' the error of the unwise,' I wonder?"

" Aye, and them people is *wilfully* ignorant," said Pat, "and would them be ' *the unlearned ?* '"

"And here's what they were wilfully ignorant about," said Jem, "about the flood that came in Noah's time, and drowned all the wicked."—(Verses 5 and 6.)

"And how would they be ignorant of that, only that they wouldn't read the Bible?" said Pat; "and sure if that's the ignorance, to not read would be the bad cure."

"Well, Pat, I'm seeing it now," said Jem; "them people *would not learn* what God did to the wicked long ago; and they *wouldn't believe* what God will do when He comes to judge the world; them's the *unlearned*, and, be-like, *unlearned* means them that *wouldn't* learn;* and, in course, them people, when the Scripture would come up against that, would have to twist that, till it didn't mean that: and isn't that the way that they would *wrest* the Scripture, hard places and easy places, to their own destruction; and doesn't that word *wrest* show that they are doing it on purpose?"

"And now look here, where he tells us *not to*

---

* Jem is right about this: the Greek word ἀμαθεῖς means those who would not be taught, and the word "unwise" in v. 17 (*wicked* in the Protestant Bible) means those who reject and despise laws, ἄθεσμον. So the *wilfully ignorant* in verse 5, those *who will not be taught*, in verse 16, and those *who despise laws*, in verse 17, are three different descriptions of the same persons.

be ignorant," said Pat, pointing to the 8th verse, "and see how he makes it out that God isn't breaking his word about coming, but only waiting to save sinners.; and see what things he tells them will be when Christ comes, when the fire will burn up the world itself and everything in it; and see here, won't there be new heavens and a new earth according to his promises, in which justice dwelleth; and look, if it isn't here, that it's looking for the new heavens and the new earth that will make us diligent, that we may be found undefiled and unspotted to him in peace."

"Is there any one at all looking for *a new earth*, Pat ?" said Jem.

"I never heard tell of it before," said Pat, "and how would I look for it ?"

"Nor I neither," said Jem.

"Nor none of the people in this country," said Pat.

"And doesn't St. Peter say we shouldn't be ignorant of it ?" said Jem.

"And why should we be ignorant of it if it's that that's to make us diligent ?" said Pat.

"And yet it's one of the hard things surely," said Jem.

"And yet St. Peter writes about it to all them people in all them countries ; and to the servants too," said Pat.

"And where he was talking about hard things, he's just telling them hard things himself," said Jem.

"And maybe if things is hard, there's more call for the Apostles themselves to teach us about them," said Pat.

"And maybe the hardness is in the things,* more nor in writing about them," said Jem.

"And maybe no one else could speak half as plain or as sure about them," said Pat.

"Anyway, he wasn't wanting to keep the hard things off of them," said Jem.

"And it wasn't by talking to them, but just by writing to them about the hard things, for them to read it, that he wanted to keep them right," said Pat.

"Why, if he talked it to them, that might be easy forgot ; and they mightn't know easy, ten years after, just what it was he said," said Jem.

---

* Jem is quite right about this. The Greek makes it quite plain that the Apostle meant, in which *things* (not in which *epistles*) there are some things hard to be understood—that is, in the coming of Christ, and the burning of the world, and the new heavens and the new earth, there are things hard to be understood.

"And if he only talked it to them, how would *we* get knowing what he said exactly? but when he wrote it, that does for always," said Pat.

"Maybe if he only spoke it to them, it would get about wrong; and maybe some people would allow that he said the Bible was hard, and bid us not read it," said Jem.

"Maybe if he only spoke it, and didn't write it, *that* would be the tradition in the Church of Rome now," said Pat.

"Well, that it would, with Father John anyway," said Jem; "but St. Peter spoiled that entirely by writing it."

"Well, and now for the caution he put on it all," said Pat.

"Aye," said Jem, "he bid them take heed——"

"Stop a bit, Jem," said Pat; "I mind now them words is in it before, if we can only come on them and put them together, and see how they fit."

But Pat could not find the words, though he was sure he saw them somewhere; so Jem tried *his* book, and he found them in chap. i. verse 19. So they put the two books together again, and Jem said, "Well, it's *take heed* in my book, and it's *attend* in yours, and sure that's all one ; and what did he bid them attend to ?"

" Well, it's *the firm prophetical word* in one book, and it's *the sure word of prophecy* in the other ; and what's that ?" said Jem.

"Sure that would be what the prophets wrote in the Old Testament," said Pat.

" Well," said Jem, " I didn't read much of that, for I found it a deal harder than the New Testament, so I let it alone ; but see here if St. Peter doesn't say of that, ' whereunto *you do well to attend,* as to a light that shineth in a dark place, until the day dawn, and the day star arise in your hearts ?' and didn't he write the letter to servants and all ?"

"Then, maybe, if we attend to the hard places, there will light come out of them yet," said Pat.

" Anyway, he bid them attend well to the Bible, in the very same letter in which he bid them take heed, lest they should be led away by the error of the unwise," said Jem ; "and sure that wasn't bidding them not read the Bible ?"

" It seems it's them that won't think or learn about Christ's coming to judgment that's in danger to wrest the Scriptures wrong," said Pat ;

"but them that's still thinking of that day more nor of this day is to attend to the Scriptures, or how would they know about that day ?"

"Well, St. Peter said the great thing about knowledge here," said Jem, and he read the second verse in the first chapter (Ep. 2.)— "Grace to you and peace be accomplished *in the knowledge of God and of Christ Jesus our Lord.*"

"And where will we get that knowledge if we don't in the Bible ?" said Pat ; "wasn't I going to mass for forty years, and knowing nothing ? and will I let anyone tell me that I didn't learn more about God and Christ since I took to the reading the Bible than ever I did in them forty years ? Don't I know about the praty and the stone ? don't I know about the hen ? don't I know about the door ? don't I know about the Mediator ? don't I know about the blood of Christ ? don't I know that them that asks will get, and them that seeks will find ? but what signifies talking ? won't I keep to the reading ?"

"Well, Pat," said Jem, "we have got nothing again the reading yet."

And if ever they do we will tell it fairly.

CHAPTER XIX.

THE LONG CAR.

"WELL, Pat, my man, any news of Kiloommon those times?" said Jem.

"There is, Jem," said Pat, "for I was in on Monday."

"And how is matters getting on there?" said Jem.

"Why, then it's all getting mighty quiet," said Pat, "and the readers just able to go about like any one else; and I wouldn't see any stir at all there, maybe, only for the long car."

"And what of the long car, Pat," said Jem; "what call had that to the readers, anyway?"

"Why, there was a gentleman out of England stopping at Mr. Owens', and the word was gone about that it was him sent the readers to Kilcommon, and to all Ireland, and that he was come to look after them; and, sure enough, when the long car came in, he was waiting for a seat on it; and word went about that it was himself that was in it. Well, it was market day—and the big market it was, coming on Christmas; and I seen the town sergeant, in his blue coat and red collar, giving the people the wink, and them gathering round the car, and the gentleman on it ; and they had the children in the front, and the girls and boys behind them, and the women behind them, and the men at the back of all (for that's the plan), and they all screeching 'souper,' and 'jumper,' and 'devil,' and all the names they have, at the gentleman on the car ; and all the noises of the market going on too ; for there was Ned Kelly, the ragman, singing the ould song ' Tear away, tear away ! haul away, tear away !' and Mr. Plunket, the auctioneer, standing on the cart, selling the shawls and gowns, and the people screeching and making all the horrid noises ever you heard. And there was an old mare in the long car, that was a wee thought 'maggotty,' and she wouldn't go a step with the people screeching fornenst her ; and when Billy Donaghy, that was driving, fell to laying it into her, she turned to, lashing at him ; and it beat all, entirely. Well, then, Mr. Plunket, that's always setting the people on against the readers, took to canting the souper, when he seen there was no one bidding for the shawls ; so says he, 'Going, going, going,' says he, 'a fine fat souper going—

for one quart of soup !' So the people fell to shouting more nor ever ; and old Billy Donaghy took to flattering them—'Oh, boys,' says he, 'sure you won't see me kilt entirely ? Won't yees be easy one minute, till I get her away ? Sure it's the devil's in the mare,' says he. 'You're a liar,' says the boys, 'it's the devil's on the car,' says they, 'and it's a rale Catholic mare she is ; better nor you,' says they, 'to be driving what's on the car.' Well, with that, as if there wasn't noise enough, up comes Nick Flaherty that sells the ballads, with a new song all in strips over his arm, and him calling it through the market, 'Only wan hapeny, for St. Patrick's hymn, only wan hapeny,' and then he fell to singing it, and of all the songs ever you heard for St. Patrick, it was the quare one ; but only one verse stuck to me, and it was what St. Patrick was preaching to the heathens in Ireland :—

> Have done with your fighting,
> And think of your sins,
> Or I'll break every bone
> In your impudent skins.*

'St. Patrick's hymn, only wan hapeny' ; well, just then, the police came up, and they cleared

* If any of our readers in the neighbourhood of Navan could get a copy of this song for us, we should be obliged.—Ed.

the way for the old mare, and the gentleman
stood up on the car, and he takes off his hat,
and gives it a whirl round his head, and says he,
' Now, boys, one cheer more before we go ;' so,
with that, they all fell to laughing and cheering
him, for a pleasant gentleman he was ; so the
long car drove off in the height of good humour.
And I'm thinking, maybe that's the last of the
bad noises in Kilcommon ; for it's all getting
quiet now, in spite of Father John and Mr.
Plunket, and the town sergeant, too."

"Well, Pat," said Jem, "it's time for it to
stop, for it was disgracing us all ; and sure the
people wouldn't keep it up for ever, though
they'd be put up to it for a while. But sure
that was the quare song for St. Patrick. I
wonder what Father John would say to that."

"And what would he say to it ?" said Pat,
"sure isn't it the very moral for himself. Sure
don't I remember, afore the famine, when the
people used to be kneeling in the chapel-yard, at
mass ; and don't I mind it as regular as the day
came, how Father John, or one of the curates,
would go the rounds of the chapel-yard, with the
horsewhip, to keep the boys and girls to their
duties, and all the people in the street and the

houses forenint the chapel looking on ? And wouldn't it be just the moral for Father John, if that *was* the way St. Patrick did speak to the heathens ? But, I doubt if St. Patrick was a Protestant, as Mr. Owen says he was, he didn't do the likes of that at all ; for sure, the Protestants doesn't do them things."

"Well, Pat," said Jem, "them times is past anyway ; the people is got past that, and they wouldn't stand it now ; and I don't see the horsewhip with the priests at all now, barring of an odd time at an election, or a fight, or the like of that."

"Well, it's small call they have for it in the chapel-yard anyway," said Pat ; "for you might play ball in the chapel itself, and the people in it."

"And is the readers doing anything in Kilcommon ?" said Jem.

"Well, I hear there's a deal of people talking to them now, Jem," said Pat, "and there's a deal of people goes to the controversial class now ; and I went there myself that night."

"And what were they talking about ?" said Jem.

"Well, it was about the Mass," said Pat ;

"but you would never think, Jem, what came uppermost."

" And what was it at all ?" said Jem.

" Why, it was about the candles on the altar, Jem," said Pat.

" Well, was not there more in it to talk about than that, Pat ?" said Jem.

" Well, there's more depending to the candles nor you think, may be," said Pat.

" Well, tell us all about that, Pat," said Jem.

" Why, the Rev. Mr. Burke (that's the missioner) he put it to them, was the wafer turned into the body and blood of Christ, and his soul and divinity too, when the priest said the words over it ; and then up gets Mickey Reilly, the schoolmaster, that's a very learned man, and says— 'Sure it is,' says he, 'for they're the words of Christ, and won't His word always do what He means?' says he. 'And does it *always* happen when the priest speaks the word over the bread?' says Mr. Burke. 'Surely it does,' says Mickey. 'When the word of Christ is spoken over the bread how can it fail?' says he. 'And did you never hear of *defects* in the Mass?' says Mr. Burke. 'How could there be defects in the Mass,' says Mickey, 'when it depends on the

word of Christ, that can't fail?' says he.
'There's no defects in the Mass nor couldn't be,'
says he; 'but that's the way the Protestants are
always speaking, for they can't make an act of
faith, and they can't believe that Christ's word
will always do its work; but the Catholics that
can make an act of faith knows that there can't
be no defects in the Mass,' says he. So the Rev.
Mr. Burke takes out a book with a fine red cover,
and plenty of gold on it, and 'What book is
that?' says he. 'It's the Mass Book,' says Mickey
Reilly, when he looked at it. 'Is it the real Mass
Book?' says Mr. Burke. 'It is,' says he, 'and
no mistake.' 'Do you know the Latin?' says
Mr. Burke. 'I do,' says he. So Mr. Burke
opened a place, and says he, 'Will you read that
to the meeting in English?' So Mickey read
out mighty clever, 'It's about the defects in the
celebration of the Mass,' says he. Well, with
that all the Catholics that was there began to
look mighty quare; and Mickey read on, that
'a defect might occur in the thing that was to be
consecrated, or the form that was used, or in the
minister himself; and if there is any defect in
them, there's no sacrament made,' says he, 'and
sure enough your reverence is right, and knows

more about the Mass Book than I do,' says he.
And so Mr. Burke just takes the book and turns
to another page, and bids him read that ; so says
Mickey, 'It's about defects occurring in the
ministering itself,' says he : and then Mr. Burke
puts his finger on a place, and Mickey reads—
'If there be not *wax* candles present,' says he ;
'sure enough,' says he, 'it won't do without the
wax by this,' says he; 'and if the candles isn't
wax it's a defect, and the sacrament isn't made
at all,' says he; so with that up jumps Barney
Daly, and, says he : 'Now I know all about it,
your reverence,' says he. 'About what ?' says
Mr. Burke. 'About what Father John said to
the Boord of Guardians,' says he. 'And what
was that ?' said Mr. Burke. 'Why, I was in
the poorhouse,' says he, 'the times was so hard,
and the Master put me over one of the wards ;
and he wanted me afore the Boord one day,
about some business ; and while I was waiting
in the boord-room, in comes Father John, and
whispers the Clerk, and says the Clerk to the
Chairman, his reverence wants to address the
Boord, so the Chairman says they was ready to
hear him. So Father John says he wanted wax
candles for the Mass, for he couldn't do it with

tallow any longer.* So there was some talk about it, but in course they gave Father John what he wanted, for the Boord always does that; and the wax candles were given from that day out; for the Master still sent me for them. But now, your Reverence, what came of all them people that was going to the Mass for all them years in the poorhouse, and him doing it with the dips?' So Mr. Burke turned round on Mickey Reilly, 'and what do you say to that?' says he; 'does it depend on the word of Christ only, or does it depend on the wax too?' 'Well, your reverence,' said Mickey, 'that's the sorest thing I heard again the Mass yet.' 'And isn't it the poor thing, your Reverence,' says Barney Daly, 'to have to worship the Host, and we having no way to know for sure and certain what it is, at all? How did I know what I was worshipping in the poorhouse? How did I know was it the body and blood and soul and divinity of Christ, or was it only just a wafer I was worshipping? and it all depending on the wax or the tallow, and I knowing nothing about

* It is a fact that about the time mentioned the priests did make this demand in many workhouses. It was just after the missionaries to Roman Catholics had called their attention to this defect in the Mass.

that, or Father John neither, till it was put in his head by the Protestants, maybe? And isn't it the poor thing to be worshipping we don't know what?' says he. 'So then,' says Mr. Burke, 'what does Christ say about that?' says he. So then I spoke up, and says I, 'Didn't Christ say to the woman, " you adore that which you know not; we adore that which we know" (John, chap. iv., verse 22); and,' says I, ' mustn't we learn from Christ what we ought to adore, and did he ever tell us to adore the bread and wine that he blessed?' and Mr. Burke allowed that was right. And then says some one, ' What candles had Christ at all when he instituted the sacrament?' 'No candles at all,' says Mr. Burke, 'only lamps; for,' says he, there was no candles made in the world at that time.' And you'll think it quare, Jem, to hear how he proved that; 'for,' says he, 'there was a city just covered over with ashes and cinders out of a burning mountain, just soon after the time of our Saviour, and it was dug out not long ago, and all the houses found, and the people's bones, and their duds, just all as they left them, and not a sign of so much as a tin candlestick, let alone a brass one, found in one of them, only lamps that wouldn't burn wax at all; and if they had candles, wouldn't they have some kind of candlesticks to hold them in?"*

"Well, Pat," said Jem, "maybe that's true, but what signifies it? sure if the Word of God was to do it all, wouldn't it do by tallow-light as well as by wax-light? Sure that shows it isn't all right anyway."

"Well, there was more nor that, too," said Pat. "Sure Mr. Burke showed us out of the same mass-book that there was twenty other things by their own showing that would stop the sacrament being made, and things that we couldn't know nothing about; for sure one of them is, if the wine is sour; and how would we know that, when we don't taste it? and then there's no sacrament made at all; or if the priest isn't minding what he's at, or if he looks off the book when he says the words; and how can we tell about them things at all? and now, Pat,

* This applies to two cities buried under the eruptions of Mount Vesuvius, soon after the time of Christ, and dug out in the last century; Herculaneum and Pompeii. The word translated "candle" in the Bible does not necessarily mean such candles as we have. The Greek word is λυχνον, and the Latin *lucerna.* The most exact translation is "a light." The learned Roman Catholic, Calmet, says the "candlestick" in the Temple was, in fact, a lamp—See his Dictionary of the Bible, at the word "Lamp." Moses says it was oil that was used in this "candlestick"—see Levit. xxiv. 2—4.

how do we know at all *what* we were worshipping at the mass?"

"Well, Jem," said Pat, "I'm sure Christ would not leave us that way, not to know what we were worshipping. But, sure, don't we know he never told the Apostles to worship the bread and wine at all, but only to eat and drink it? and if we keep to what he said, why need we trouble ourselves about what anyone said afterwards?"

"That's it, Pat," said Jem; "if we stick to that we can't be astray."

So we hope to tell yet what that brought them to in the end.

CHAPTER XX.

THE MAN BEHIND THE DOOR.

"Sore weather, Pat, for the creatures that hasn't the turf," said Jem, when they met in the snow.

"And mighty hard on some poor old-fashioned creatures that hasn't any little praties they had out of the ground yet," said Pat.

"Well, there's not many that lazy now, Pat," said Jem.

"'Deed," said Pat, "the old song is nearly out now, and time for it ; you mind that, Jem :

> First there was three weeks of frost,
> And then there was three weeks of snow ;
> And the praties was like to be lost
> For want of a moderate thow.

"Ay, Pat," said Jem, "I mind having to sing that myself in old times. But the people is getting to look after things better, since trouble came on them. And not one thing alone ; for aren't we learning to look after the Bread of life too ?"

"But what will we do at all, Jem, about that man behind the doore ?" said Pat.

"Why, then, I'm thinking, Pat," said Jem,

were not ripe," said Mr. Burke, "then, the mass-book itself allows there would be no sacrament made at all, and the people would be worshipping only plain bread and wine."

" And how would we know if the grapes were ripe ? " said Pat.

" Well, now that's worse again," said Jem; " why, if it was only the candles, sure we could see that for ourselves, if they were made of the right thing.   But how will we ever know at all whether the wine was made of ripe grapes? Sure we can't taste it, and if we did itself, it's hard for the like of us to be judges of that."

" And maybe the priest might be a bad judge of wine himself, too," said Mr. Burke, "and then only think what might happen, even if the mass-book is right."

" But how will we know if your reverence is right this time," said Pat, scratching his head; " sure you were wrong about the mass-book last time, and how will we know if you be right now ?"

" Oh, Pat," said Jem, " haven't we the right way to know about it now ?   Sure won't we just take it to the man behind the doore, and see what he can say again it ? "

"Quite right," said the Rev. Mr. Burke, "that's just what we want; that everything we say should be examined : and have we not asked the priests to come and hear what we say, and to correct as much as they can of it. And you may be sure they would do it if they could. I would rather you went to the priest and asked him about what I say of the wine; but if you cannot do that, just ask the man behind the door."

"Well, your reverence," said Jem, "it's better and better; for sure *we* durstn't go to ask the priest; but, sure enough, the man behind the door can ask the priest; and won't the priest put *him* up to all he can ? So now we are just in the right way to get satisfaction about everything."

So they were going away to look for the man behind the door; but Mr. Burke stopped them for a little more talk about candles.

"And," said Mr. Burke, "what about kissing the candles, boys ?"

"Anan, your reverence," said Pat.

"What about kissing the candles ?" said Mr. Burke.

it, but not the hand of the priest. The celebrant also kisses it on receiving it, and afterwards presents it to the sub-deacon, who receives it with the ordinary kisses, and deposits it on the altar. The celebrant, having afterwards taken another candle," &c. ; and so the kissing goes on.

"And, your reverence, was that always done in the Church?" said Pat.

"Well, I suppose," said Mr. Burke, "it could not be older than the blessing of candles ou Candlemass-day."

"And how old is that?" said Pat.

"Here is a book, written by a very learned Roman Catholic, who searched for that," said Mr. Burke ; "and he says he could find nothing about it in any of the service-books of any Church for 900 years after Christ. But stay," said Mr. Burke, "the man behind the door might say I was wrong, so I will write it out for you to give him ;" so he wrote them a paper which we will print at the end of this chapter.

"And will your reverence tell us what are blessed candles good for?" said Jem.

"I cannot tell you much about that," said Mr. Burke. "This book * says, indeed (p. 233), that

* "The Ceremenial," mentioned above.

in lesser churches the priest 'sits upon a seat prepared upon the gospel side (of the altar), covers, and gives an instruction to the people upon the institution of this solemnity, upon the mystic significations *and the advantages of blessed candles;*' but the book does not give the discourse, so I cannot tell what is in it. All I know about it is from a form of blessing candles printed at the end of the mass-book (p. xcvii.), where the priest prays over them thus :—' . . . Let them (the candles) receive such a benediction by the sign of the holy cross, that in whatever places they are lighted or placed, the princes of darkness may depart, and tremble, and fly in consternation, with all their ministers, from those habitations; nor presume any more to disquiet or molest those who serve thee, the Omnipotent God.' "

"And what does your reverence think of that prayer ?" said Jem.

"I think," said Mr. Burke, "that God hears the prayer of faith ; and the prayer of faith must be *founded* on the *word or promise* of God. St. James says (ch. iv. 7, Douay Bible), 'Resist the devil, and he will fly from you ;' and St. Peter himself says of the devil, ' whom resist ye, strong in faith' (1 Peter, v. 9). These are God's promises of driving away the devil; but no Apostle says, 'light candles to drive away the devil.' If we resist him and pray to God to accomplish his own promise, *that* is the prayer of faith that God will hear; but if we light candles, and pray that candles may drive away the devil, *that* prayer rests on human inventions; it has no promise from God; it cannot be the prayer of faith."

"Well, your reverence," said Jem, "I think that's right; and if blessed candles was the thing to keep away the enemy of souls, would Christ and his Apostles have left his Church *without them* for NINE HUNDRED YEARS ?"

So Pat and Jem were going away, when Mr. Burke called out to them—"Will you go and buy blessed candles now ?" And Pat answered him—"Your reverence, I would rather put the money in a Douay Bible: doesn't Christ himself say, 'I am the light of the world; he that followeth me walketh not in darkness, but shall have the light of life'? and wasn't that said before there was any blessed candles at all ? And isn't *that* better nor candles ?"—John viii. 12.

So as they were going out of the door, Mr.

Burke said, " Now, be sure you show the paper to the man behind the door, and tell him every word I said."

" Never fear, your reverence," said Pat ; " we will surely."

The paper given by Mr. Burke to Pat, to show to " the man behind the door."

" De benedictione cereorum nulla fit mentio apud Amalarium, Valfridum, et vulgatum Alcuinum, qui cereos tantum a Pontifice dari asserit. Sed neque in Gelasiano, Gregoriano, Gellonensi, aliisqe supra nongentas annos scriptis sacramentariis aliquid ea de re extat. In antiquo missali ecclesiæ Turonensis ante annos 800 scripto unica *ad luminaria benedicenda* reperitur" . . —(Tractatus de antiqua ecclesiæ Disciplina, &c.," by Edmund Martene, a Benedictine monk. Edit. Lugdun, 1706 ; p. 117).

Which we thus translate, for the convenience of our readers :

" Concerning the *blessing* of wax candles, *no mention is made* in Amalarius, Walfrid, or the Vulgate copy of Alcuin, who only states that wax candles were *given* by the Pope ; neither in the Gelasian, or Gregorian Sacramentaries, or in that at Gello, or in others, written above 900 years ago, is there any mention made about that matter.   In an ancient missal of the Church of Tours, written 800 years ago (*i.e.*, about 906), one only mention is found about blessing candles."[*]

CHAPTER XXI.

THE DUMMY.

"WELL, Jem," said Pat, "I had a talk with a neighbour, and I want to tell it to you."

"Well, Pat, let us hear it," said Jem.

"Well, Jem," said Pat, "it was with Neddy Boylan, about the Readers and the Bible; and Neddy allowed it was just folly for the people to be listening to them at all; 'for sure,' says he, aren't we better as we are?'   Well, with that I asked him was the Bible the Word of God at all?   And he allowed there was no saying again

---

[*] "The man behind the door" had written a letter to the Editor of the *Catholic Layman* (in which the Talk of the Road first appeared), pointing out the distinction between those defects of the Mass which nullify it and those that do not (see *Catholic Layman*, vol. 3, p. 10); but he never referred again to the subject of wax candles or sour grapes after the publication of the above chapter.

that.   And then I asked him wouldn't the
religion that agreed with the Word of God be
better than the religion that was against it.
Well, he allowed that, too; 'and now,' says I,
'what way have you for knowing that the
priest's religion is better, by the Word of God,
than the parson's? Sure the priest won't let you
look into the Bible to see if his religion is in it;
and doesn't the parson offer to *show* you *his* in
the Bible; and doesn't that itself look as if the
parson had the best of it by the Bible?' 'Well,'
says he, 'maybe it does, for that matter; but I
don't want to know nothing at all about it; sure
ain't I better as I am?' says he.   'Arrah, man,'
says I, 'do you mean to tell me that it is better
not to know which religion is true than to know
it?' 'Well,' says he, 'if I don't know it, isn't it
the priest's look out,' says he; 'and if I did
know it, wouldn't it be my own look out,' says
he; 'and so ain't I better as I am,' says he,
'knowing nothing about it at all?' 'And do
you mean to tell me,' says I, 'that if your
religion is not the right way of salvation, that it's
the priest will be damned instead of you, and you
get salvation without being in the right way for
it?' 'And do you mean to tell me,' says he,

' that God will lay all the blame on me, that knows nothing at all about it myself, and only just does what the priest bids me, that *ought* to know better nor ever I can know ? And,' says he, 'don't you mind Pat Brady, that has the son that's a dummy, and innocent, and didn't Pat teach the creature to steal praties ? and when them both was up afore the Bench for it, didn't the magistrates say they wouldn't punish the dummy creature at all, 'cause he didn't know nothing at all ; and they laid all the punishment on the man that taught him, and he knowing nothing himself, the creature ; and do you mean to tell me,' says he, ' that the merciful God will be harder on the poor creatures that knows nothing, and only does as they are bid, than the magistrates was? Sure I won't believe that at all,' says he. ' Well,' says I, ' Neddy (when I considered a bit), it doesn't seem to me to be like that at all. Sure the dummy *couldn't* know the differ of what was right or wrong ; and sure it's you that *won't* know it, Neddy,' says I, ' and sure that's not the same at all ; and sure, Neddy,' says I, ' if you was to go and be a dummy on purpose, and to try to make your own self a fool, the way you could steal praties, sure the magistrates wouldn't let *you* off for THAT, Neddy. I'm thinking it's the worse they'd give it to you, if they knew that you *wouldn't* know the differ of right and wrong, Neddy,' says I. 'And how *would* I know the differ if there's no one to teach me,' says he ; 'and sure isn't it a Souper I'd be called if I would ask the priest to teach me out of the Bible ?' says he. 'Well, sure enough, it was that way long enough,' says I ; 'but it isn't that way now ; for sure there's Mr. Owens, and there's the readers that's come, all willing and ready to show us that their religion is in the Bible ; and now, if the priest will just do the same, sure then we can see for ourselves what religion is in the Word of God.' 'Well, that's just it,' says he, 'and that's just the reason why I wish the readers was hunted out of the country,' says he. 'And how would you know then,' says I, 'which religion is true ?' 'And isn't that just what I don't want to know ?' says he. 'Sure,' says he, 'before the readers came, weren't we just as safe as the dummy, not knowing nothing, and not having no way of knowing nothing, and weren't we quite quiet and easy ; and now,' says he, 'every time the readers pass my door, don't I feel that they are just putting it on myself to

know what religion is right, and just leaving me
with no excuse for putting it all on the priest;
and now,' says he, 'weren't we better as we
were? and why would the readers be coming
here to put it all on ourselves, when it wasn't on
ourselves before?' 'Well, Neddy,' says I, 'by
that way of reckoning, wouldn't it be the fine
thing if Jesus Christ had never come into the
world at all to show us the way of salvation?'
'And how's that?' says he; 'sure I didn't go for
to say the like of that at all?' 'Well,' says I,
'sure we could all say then that we knew nothing
at all about what religion was true, and that we
hadn't no way to know; and sure we could put
it all on Adam, that sinned; and on God, too,
that let us be born in sin, and gave us no
knowledge; and sure if it's a fine thing to know
nothing,' says I, 'wouldn't that be the way we
would know nothing at all; and wouldn't it
be the finest of all?'. 'Well, I didn't mean
that,' says he; 'but sure the readers is putting it on me to know for myself, and sure it
wasn't put on me before?' 'And didn't Jesus
Christ, when He came into the world, put it on
people to know Him, and to judge for themselves
that it was Him? and didn't He put it on them

to know if his religion was true ? and didn't He put it on them to search the Scriptures to find out if it was Him that was in it ? and didn't He put it on them to repent, and to turn to Him, and to believe in Him ? and why wouldn't the Word of God do just the same now,' says I, ' when it comes to our own doors ?' So I seen he was studying, and he couldn't get over that ; so, says I to him, ' Neddy, says I, ' just tell me, *was it worse* for the people then, for Jesus Christ, the Saviour of the world, to come to them ?' ' Well,' says he, ' I don't know what to say to it, and I would like for somebody to tell me.' ' Well,' says I, ' I think it was *better* for them that would hear and learn from Him, for sure they found salvation,' says I ; 'and I'm thinking,' says I, ' it *was worse* for them that *wouldn't* learn, for sure then they had no excuse,' says I ; and with that I just got out my Bible before he could stop me, and I showed him what Jesus Christ said Himself—'This is the judgment, because the Light is come into the world, and men loved darkness rather than the light' (John, iii. 19, Douay Bible). 'And is it that way with the readers ?' says he. 'Well, it was that way with the Apostles,' says I ; 'for here is what St. Paul says of himself and the rest of them—"We are the good odour of Christ unto God, in them that are saved, and in them that perish ; to the one, indeed, we are the odour of death unto death, but to the others the odour of life unto life."' (2 Cor. ii. 15 and 16.)　'And is it that way with the readers?' says he.　'It's that way,' says I, 'with the word that Jesus Christ spoke, and that's in the Bible ; so I'm thinking,' says I, 'it's always that way with them that offers to show us the Word of God.'　'Well, that's just what was angering me against the readers,' says he. 'Take care that same wouldn't anger you against the Word of God,' says I.　'I doubt it would,' says he, 'if I gave in to it any more.'　'Well, don't,' says I ; 'sure it's come to your door now, and you can't put it away if you would : just turn to it,' says I, 'and see if it isn't for life and salvation to them that receives it.'　'That's what I'll have to do,' says he, 'and I knew myself it would come to that,' says he, "cause I was angry at it ;' so there's my story, Jem."

"And a good story, too, Pat," said Jem ; "you handled it well ; and I believe there's a deal of people in the country that has got that notion ; they *feel* the readers is putting it on themselves to know what religion is true, and they don't feel yet that it is the knowledge of the way of salvation that the readers is putting on them. But I suppose, Pat, it be to be that way at first; and sure it's something when the people begins to feel that itself; for, sure, when that begins to work in them a bit, they won't be able to turn it off. But did you ask the man behind the door, Pat, about what the Rev. Mr. Burke said of the wine that wasn't made of ripe grapes? and what did you get out of him?"

"Oh, just not one word, said Pat. "I knew he was there, and I shouted it to him, and he heard it all, and wouldn't say one word, good nor bad."

"Well, that's enough, Pat," said Jem; "Mr. Burke is right this time, anyway."

So they went home for that night, and, no doubt, will be talking again.

———

CHAPTER XXII.

THE IRISH IN AMERICA.

"WELL, Jem, what's the talk about now?" said Pat.

"America letters, Pat," said Jem.

"Signs by, you got one, Jem," said Pat.

"'Deed, then, I did, from my daughter, Biddy, that went out a year ago; and the good daughter she is, sending me two pounds to put wee duds on the childer; and she'll send more when she gets it," said Jem.

"Well, America is the fine place," said Pat. "Sure, it's long till she would make that here."

"There's a deal that does well there, Pat," said Jem; "but, I doubt, there's a deal too that goes there, and wishes themselves home again."

"Well, I never heard tell of that, Jem," said Pat; "there's hardly an America letter I hear of but has money in it." •

"Aye, Pat," said Jem, "sure enough, the creatures write when there's money to send; but then there's a deal that never writes at all, and that's more like as if they had nothing than as if they forgot them they left in Ireland."

"Well, that's true, I'm sure," said Pat, "for sure it's good for the heart to think how them that goes remembers them that is left; and I marked that often, that them that doesn't write or send money is seldom heard of in the neighbours' letters. But how comes it, Jem, that they wouldn't write?"

"Well, Pat," said Jem, "I heard something of that, and I mind it well. A while back I was waiting for the railway at Glasson, and there was a nice old gentleman standing on the platform, talking to a man ; and he *was* a gentleman to look at, for his face looked as if it had seen all weathers, and his long white hair, and his clear gray eyes, that looked as if they had seen all the world ; and the life there was in that old man, you would wonder to see it in one so old. And it was about *that* he was talking, how it came that so many that went there out of Ireland didn't write home ; it was about the years of the famine and the fever he was talking, how the creatures took out the fever with them in the ships ; and there was an island in America that was turned into an hospital, and all the ships had to put the people there ; and he was there in the island, and I'm thinking maybe he was taking care of them, and I hope he was, for he was a kindly-feeling gentleman ; and I heard him tell how he seen ninety-six of them buried in one grave. And to hear him speaking, and him striking his stick on the ground, you.would think the dead was rising up again afore his face, and him speaking. And it just come into my mind then, it was no wonder there was so many that was never heard tell on more ; for sure the old mothers and the sweethearts in Ireland might think long afore they would get word nor tidings of the poor boys and girls that was buried in that grave."

"Well, that's the sad story, Jem," said Pat, "but sure, I mind myself, when Johnny Davis, the whitesmith, went out with his wife and the five children—and they all took the fever, and went to hospital—and maybe it was in that island ; and when he got well, and found them all dead, he just took his passage by the next ship, and came home to the old forge, a lone and sorrowful man ; and I mind well the words I heard him say—'I went out full, and the Lord hath brought me home again empty ;' but I don't know were them words his own, or where did he get them."

"Well, I can tell you that, Pat," said Jem ; "he got them words in the Book of Ruth, in the Bible, the beautifullest and feelingest story that ever was told ; nothing could beat it ; and I'm often thinking there's nothing can come across us but we'll find the right words for that in the Bible, if we only knew where to look for it ; and that story of Ruth is worth your reading; it goes to the heart clean."

"Well, I'll look for that next, Jem," said Pat; "but sure when we do hear of them that goes to America, isn't it the blessed thing to hear how they think of them they left in Ireland, and how good they are to them, and how they think long of the old country and the old places. I mind now, when I went up to Meath, with some cattle, last spring, and I just called in to see Biddy Farrelly, that's my mother's brother's daughter, and she showed me a letter she got from Mary Brady, that's a cousin of hers; and Mary was gone out two years, and was doing well, and she said she wanted to get married; but there wasn't a Meath boy in all that country she was in, and she said she would never marry none but a Meath boy; so she just writes home to Biddy Farrelly (for she knew that Biddy had the good heart), and she tells her to look out for a Meath boy that's a good son, and didn't drink, and she sends home seven pound ten to get him a new suit, and send him out to marry her.   So Biddy had got a clean, decent boy, in Meath, and was just sending him out, in a new suit, to be married upon Mary

Brady. And, now, doesn't it show how they think of the old place and them so far off?"

"Well, Pat," said Jem, "it does one good, surely, to know how they think of the old place; but there's one thing they learn to think of new. I hear there's a great deal of them that goes out that takes to reading the Bible. Now, I mind the letters that old Ned Flanagan showed me that he got from his daughter. Well, in the first letter he got, she told him she was in a good place and doing well; but one thing was breaking her heart, for there was no chapel, nor priest, nor Mass within thirty miles of her. So, says she, 'Father, dear, won't you try and get a Mass or two said for me in Ireland, and I will send the money to pay for them when I get it.' Well, it's little money old Ned had, and maybe he would have thought better to spend it on duds for the children that was a'most naked; but anyway he hadn't it, and so he be to wait for the masses till he got the money; for you know, Pat, 'no money no Mass.' So the next letter comes a month after, with two pounds in it to keep him and the children warm, and at the end of it, says she, 'Father, dear, there's no hurry about the Masses, and you needn't get them said till I write again.' Well, a month after there comes another letter, with more money, and says she, 'Father, dear, you needn't mind the Masses now, for I'm took to reading the Bible, and I find that better nor Masses.' So, you see the Masses were done without, Pat, after all."

"Well, Jem," said Pat, "sure we needn't go past Father John's own sermon for that, when he read us Father Mullen's letter,* out of America, and preached against any of the people going to America any more ; and told them they might as well turn Protestants at once, and sell their souls to the devil, and turn Bible-readers ; and sure he made it out that there wasn't one in ten that kept to the Church of Rome there ; but, sure enough, Jem, that didn't stop people going, for all that ; and I'm thinking there's many a one goes just for that same reason, because Father John told them there was plenty there to make it easy to do as they liked ; and now I mind what a man told me that went to Liverpool to see his daughter off to America. There's a Protestant clergyman in Liverpool,

* This letter of the Rev. Mr. Mullen, R. C. Curate of Clon-mellon, was published in the *Freeman's Journal*. He calculates the number lost to the (R.) Catholic Church in America at 1,990,000, or, in round numbers, TWO MILLIONS.

and it's just his business to attend all the America
ships that's going off; and there's a steamer that
takes all the America ships down the river, pulling them with a rope; and the clergyman goes
off with every ship, and comes back by the
steamer; and he's reading the Bible, and talking,
and praying with them as far as the steamer
goes; and this man went down with his daughter, to come back with the steamer, and there
was a priest, too, on board, but whether he was
going to America in that ship, I did not hear;
but the clergyman had them all reading the
Bible, and talking to them; and the priest was
looking mighty cross, at the end of the ship; and
at last the priest comes for'ad, and, says he to all
the people, 'Is there any Catholics there?' says
he. 'Yes, there is, severals, your reverence,'
says the people to him. 'Well,' says he, 'I
command all Catholics to go away out of this,
and not to listen to this stuff any more.' Well,
with that the clergyman spoke up, and says he,
"It's the word of God Himself that I am reading
to you, my friends, and you are going to begin
life again in the new world, and I want you to
begin it new, with the word and the blessing of
God;' and, with that, he asked them all to

kneel down, and pray with him for that blessing ; and man, woman, and child knelt down with him, and not one went away, barring the priest himself.* Now, doesn't that show that once they are out of Ireland, the people is free and willing, too, to listen to the word of God ?"

" But, Pat," said Jem, "if it's that way out of Ireland (and sure Father John himself let on that it is), why couldn't it be that way in Ireland, too ?"

"That's what I'm studying, Jem," said Pat, "and I don't see it plain yet ; but sure that's worth the studying."

And if they see their way to that, it may help other men to see it too.

*It may interest our readers to know, that we ourselves saw the letters that Pat and Jem were speaking of ; and we were present, too, when the old gentleman struck his stick on the ground, and told of the grave of the poor Irish emigrants. We hope that many of those who died may have commenced their voyage with the prayers of that Liverpool clergyman.—EDITOR.

CHAPTER XXIII.

THE GLORIES OF JOSEPH.

"JEM," said Pat, "do you mind the talk we had about the 'Glories of Mary'?"*

"I do, well, Pat," said Jem; "that won't be forgotten easy."

"Well, Jem," said Pat, "I have got a match for it anyway."

"And what is it, Pat?" said Jem.

"Why, then, it's the 'Glories of Joseph,' the husband of Mary," said Pat.

"Ay," said Jem, "and had he glories too?"

"Why, you know, in course, Jem," said Pat, "sure a man wouldn't be behind his wife, you know."

"Well but, Pat," said Jem, "it isn't the same; for sure the Blessed Virgin was the real mother of Jesus Christ, but Joseph wasn't his father."

"Well, Jem, here's the book," said Pat, pulling a little book out of his pocket, with "The Glories of St. Joseph"† printed in big letters on it.

* Chap. III.

† "Glories of St. Joseph, from the French of Father Paul Barrie. Printed by Richard Grace, Catholic Bookseller, Dublin, 1849."

"Sure enough, there it is," said Jem ; "what's coming now at all ?"

Perhaps our readers are saying just the same ; and if they read on they will know.

"Why, just listen to the sense of this, Jem," said Pat, "doesn't the book make Joseph as great as the Blessed Virgin herself? Just read this, man ;" and so Jem read, "If, therefore, she be a princess, he is a prince ; and he is also king wherever she is queen"—p. 15. "And now, Jem," said Pat, "isn't she the queen of heaven ; and isn't it plain by the book that Joseph is the king of heaven ?"

"Well, Pat, there is a big IF in that," said Jem.

"Sure there is, Jem," said Pat, "and don't I just want you to take the big IF along with you all through ? IF *she is* the Queen of heaven, sure her husband *be* to be the King."

"Well, Pat, I see it now," said Jem, "and, sure enough, there's more reason in you nor in the book; it's a great IF entirely."

"And in course, Jem," said Pat, "there's more follows on that ; read this here ;" so Jem read—"O rich Joseph, to whom God himself becomes a beggar !"—p. 16.

"Well, Pat," said Jem, "that does beat all; I wonder how any living man durst write it!"

"Well, Jem," said Pat, "sure it follows quite natural, out of the big IF: will you read this now." So Jem read—"God helps us in all necessities by St. Joseph, as by his plenipotentiary, to let us understand, that as he was subject to him in all things upon earth as to a father, *so he was the same in heaven*, granting whatever he asked"—p. 47. "Now," said Pat, "isn't Joseph king in heaven, if God himself is subject to Joseph there?"

"Oh, Pat," said Jem, "it's too bad entirely for any Christian to listen to: I wonder the Irish people does not rise up at once again such things."

"Maybe the people is waiting for the priests and bishops to rise up again such things," said Pat; "sure, it is the bishops and priests that ought to put down books that teaches such shocking things again the Christian faith."

"Well, Pat, that's past waiting for. Sure, don't I see here in the first page, that it is printed by Grace, the great Catholic bookseller, and sure, the Bishops would have only to say the word to stop it at once."

"But who ever heard the bishop or the priests say one word against such books as that, Jem?" said Pat. "Sure, they keep all that for the Bible. And, sure, look here at the end; here's all the indulgences that the popes give to every one that stands up for Joseph. Why, here's one that gives an indulgence of 300 days in purgatory to every one for every time that he prays to *Jesus, Mary, and Joseph*, all together. Why, how could the priests or the bishops go again that?"

"That's plain, Pat," said Jem; "we must quit all they say and do, to keep to Christ alone."

"Well, there's more things in it, Jem," said Pat; "Sure Jesus, Mary, and Joseph is the Trinity on earth! (pages 17 and 26); and Joseph was the handsomest man at all; why wouldn't he? Sure the book says Jesus Christ wouldn't take an ugly man to be his father, but one as handsome as himself."—page 20.

"Stop there, Pat," said Jem, "till I find what the Bible says about Jesus Christ." So Jem found it in Isaiah liii. 2,—"There is no beauty in him, nor comeliness, and there was no sightliness that we should be desirous of him." "So you see, Pat," said Jem, "the book is only inventing lies."

" Well, Jem," said Pat, "here's a place to tell
how easy devotion to St. Joseph is ; it's just the
easiest thing at all ; only a picture, or a bit of a
prayer or two. 'Deed he doesn't ask much for
all he does."

" And what does he do at all ?" said Jem.

" A deal of things," said Pat. " If there's anything lost, it's only to go to St. Joseph (p. 84),
and he'll look till he finds it ; and, sure, that
would keep him busy in Ireland itself, let alone
the rest of the world. Or if there's a match to
be made between a boy and a girl, only get St.
Joseph at it, and it's done (p. 127); and he can
put his hand to anything ; for if a girl is in love,
it's only to go to St. Joseph, and he'll put that
out of her head in nine days (p. 108) ; and if a
couple want children, Joseph's the man, though
he had none of his own (p. 128) ; and he's
the best man midwife at all (p. 127) ; and for
saving the agent from the ribbonmen he beats
the scapular all out ;* for, see, here's a story of a
man that was shot with a blunderbuss, with
thirty slugs in it, and every slug went into his
body, and three of them staid in his belly, and
one of them was beat flat on his nose, and he

* See CATHOLIC LAYMAN, vol. ii., 1853, p. 66.

wasn't a hair the worse ; and sure the men that wrote the book says, that the man that was shot told him the story himself"—p. 132.

"Well, Pat," said Jem, "I'm thinking one or other of them was a mighty great liar, and no mistake."

"Well, Jem," said Pat, "there was a convent, and no nuns going into it, and St. Joseph got them a young lady, with a good fortune, and the book says 'which favour will never be forgotten by that community.' Sure enough, it's girls with fortunes they take in, and not poor unfortunate creatures that it would be the place for."

"But, Jem, here's something that is good ; it's about the interior or spiritual life in the soul ; and it makes out this spiritual life is faith, hope, charity, religious adoration, thanksgiving, humiliation "—p. 95.

"Well, Pat," said Jem, "I think that's as true as if it was in the Bible."

"So it is, Jem," said Pat. "But see here, Jem, what the book says next." So Jem read (p. 99), "in a community of three score *religious**

---

* The word "religious" here means nuns. The passage shows how improper it is to use the word of all who are members of an order.

you will scarce find six true interior persons; and amongt a hundred religious men, or five hundred *seculars*,* it would be hard to find ten such as we speak of, who are eminent in their interior life, and make their desire of perfection their chief endeavour."

"Well, Pat," said Jem, "that's the sorest thing I heard yet again the convents and the priests; I wonder how did it get into the book at all."

"Well, maybe it isn't easy to write a book, and let no word of truth get into it at all," said Pat; "but there it's down in the book, however it got in."

So Pat went on—"Well, Jem, here's quare things; there's a great day for St. Joseph every year in Canada, and just read the story." So Jem read (p. 73)—"Also, many dozens of great rockets, twelve at a time, resting somewhile between each dozen. At the close of the evening, the governor of Quebec (accompanied with all his officers, in sight of a great number of savages, who live round the country, come to see the solemnity) puts fire to these machines; the wonderful sight whereof gives great occasion

* "Seculars" here means priests.

to the savages to honour and esteem St. Joseph,
for whom they perceive the Christians have so
great a veneration."

" Well," said Jem, "that beats all ways ever
I heard of making Christians of savages ; but I
never heard tell of it in any of the letters the
people wrote home."

" Well, I suppose it's an old story now," said
Pat ; " and sure if all the savages is converted,
there would be no more call for rockets.   But
here's a story as quare, about a lady called
Margaret de Chateau, who had a great regard
for Jesus, Mary, and Joseph ; and now read
that, Jem," said Pat.   So Jem read—" After she
was dead, she was opened, and in her heart they
found three precious stones, on which were en-
graved the three objects of her love "—p. 53.
" Now, Jem," said Pat, "do you believe there
ever was a woman that had her heart full of
little stones, just like the gizzard of an old
fowl ?"

" Well, 'deed, Pat," said Jem, "I don't believe
God Almighty ever made a woman with a
gizzard instead of a heart.   But what will the
Catholic books come to at all ?"

" Well, Jem," said Pat, " hear the advice that

the Blessed Virgin gives, however the book got at it." So Jem read (p. 219)—"Wherefore, if we desire her to advise us *what is best* TO SECURE OUR SALVATION, we cannot doubt but she will say, 'be devout to St. Joseph; love my dear spouse, St. Joseph.'"

"Oh, stop, stop, Pat," said Jem, "I can't stand it any more; to think us poor Irish is let to read such books, to set us so far astray about our salvation, and the word of the living God kept off us. Oh, doesn't it cry out against them that allows it? Will there never be no light nor knowledge from God, to them that's kept in darkness and the shadow of death?"

"Well, Jem," said Pat, "it's enough to give one a heartscald again the Church of Rome, sure enough; but I'll only look out one thing more; here's a whole chapter to explain why the worship of St. Joseph was so late getting into the Church. Why, the book says that, '*in the primitive ages no mention is made of any parti-cular devotion to this saint*' (p. 29); and it says, '*I cannot, therefore, but own that this marked devotion towards St. Joseph is only of late stand-ing*' (p. 29); and the book makes out that no one did worship Joseph for 1,400 years after

Christ (p. 30); and that was all '*for St. Joseph's greater honour*' (p. 35) ; and it allows that St. Teresa '*was the first who set up the standard of devotion to St. Joseph*' (p. 48); and, 'deed, Jem," said Pat, "when I came to that, I thought to myself, it's little call we have to trust to the saints, if they set us that far astray." ·

"Well, Pat," said Jem; "if any prays to St. Joseph after that, it's their own faults ; but how will it be with the priests that never says a word against such books, and with the bishops that doesn't stop the Catholic booksellers from printing the like ?"

Plenty of such books there are, printed and circulated for the Irish people to read instead of the Bible. And if Pat and Jem should talk of any more of them, our readers may like to hear of that too.

CHAPTER XXIV.

THE PRIESTS' MISSION.

"WELL, Pat, isn't it the quare time since I saw you to have a talk, while I was above at the railway, with hard work and fair pay ? and is there anything new at Kilcommon to talk of ? "

"'Deed, then, Jem," said Pat, "there's the new mission to talk of."

"Well, that's not new anyway," said Jem; "sure I saw that myself afore I went to the railroad."

"Well, it is new, Jem," said Pat. "Sure it's a Catholic mission that's in it."

"Is it the priests at a mission, Pat?" said Jem; "why, sure a station would be more in their way."

"Aye is it," said Pat; "five or six priests there holding a mission of their own."

"Well, Mr. Burke and Mr. Owens is making a stir among the priests anyway," said Jem; "sure that's a new thing entirely; but what was it like at all?"

"Why, the greatest confessing and preaching that ever you seen; and the chapel-yard like a fair with the booths and shops."

"And what shops at all in the chapel-yard?" said Jem.

"Why, booths and stands, all covered with jimcracks and toys, fit to bring all the children at a fair to them," said Pat.

"And do you say it's selling toys for the little children the missionaries were?" said Jem.

"Well, it wasn't just that," said Pat; "for it was toys for the *big* children they were selling."

"What sort at all?" said Jem.

"Why, there was stands there, all glittering in the sun, covered all over with little bits of tin, at halfpence a piece, with gilding on them as bright as gingerbread," said Pat.

"And what were they at all?" said Jem.

"Miraculous medals, Jem," said Pat.

"And did they work miracles?" said Jem.

"Sorrow one that I could hear of," said Pat.

"And did the people believe there was miracles on that stand, at a halfpenny a piece?" said Jem.

"Well, you see, them that bought them had to get them blessed by the missionaries, before there would be any good in them," said Pat.

"And did the missionaries say they were miraculous medals, when they were blessed?" said Jem.

So then Pat pulled a printed paper out of his pocket, and showed it to Jem, with a cross at the top, and "Jesus, Mary, and Joseph," printed under the cross, and under that again, in big letters, "RESOLUTION AT THE CLOSE OF THE MISSION," and then Jem read out of it,

"Prayer of the Miraculous Medal—O Mary, conceived without sin, pray for us who have recourse to thee;" and then Pat took out of his pocket a little bit of gilt tin, as big as a sixpence, with the prayer and the picture of the Virgin stamped upon it; "And," said Pat, "here's the miraculous medal, Jem."

So Jem turned it about in his fingers, "And," said he, "do they think the people has got no sense at all?   Sure, it's the height of impudence, it is, to call that miraculous."

"Well, I don't know, Jem," said Pat; "sure, when grown childer can be got in plenty to buy the like of that for a miraculous medal, it's a'most a miracle itself."

"Well, if bits of tin can beat the Bible in the long run, I'll call *that* a miracle, *when I see it*," said Jem.   "But *did* the people take to the medals, Pat?"

"Well, there was lots and lashings of them sold," said Pat; "but I don't think them that got them cared a deal for them; sure I was in Mr. Thomas's bread shop, when a boy come in, and said he had no money, and asked to buy a bit of bread with a miraculous medal, blest and all; and, indeed, Mr. Thomas gave him the bread, and took the medal, so one medal was worth something anyway."*

"And what was the preaching like, Pat?" said Jem.

"Well, it wasn't like Father John's preaching at all," said Pat; "for they didn't abuse nor blackguard nobody, not even the Scripture-readers; but kept speaking to the people about their sins, and about death and judgment, and heaven and hell, quite solemn and serious, till you'd think that the people was just frightened out of their lives, and ready to look for salvation entirely; and you would see the people's hearts was stirred up in them entirely, for they never heard the like of that preaching in the chapel before; and I'm thinking, if Father John doesn't mend his hand and try something more Christian-like, he won't go down with the people at all, after that."

"And, Pat, when the people was stirred up to look for salvation," said Jem, "did the missionaries show them the way of salvation, or did they tell them of the blood of Christ at all?"

"Not one word about it at all, Jem," said Pat.

* This did actually happen in the shop of a Protestant.

" They just stirred up the people till you would think their minds couldn't be quiet at all about their sins, and then they just left them in the lurch, and didn't give them nothing to make their peace with God."

" And was there nothing about Jesus Christ, the Saviour of sinners, then ?" said Jem.

" Nothing at all," said Pat. " There was plenty said then for the priests, but nothing at all for Christ, the Saviour of sinners ! Sure, look at this paper I showed you," said Pat: " here's about death and judgment, and heaven and hell ; and here's the Blessed Virgin six times over, and *the prayer of the miraculous medal*, and plenty of real good advice, and not one word about Jesus Christ, the Saviour, good or bad, first or last ; and *that's the priests' mission*, Jem."

So Jem read the paper over, and he could not find one word about Christ, the Saviour of sinners, in it ; and we print that paper (for a copy was sent to us) that our readers may try if they can find anything about Christ in it.

" Well," said Jem, " I think I see now what can come of it."

" And what's that, Jem ?" said Pat.

" Well, it's my opinion,"said Jem, " that them

that's stirred up to think of their sins, and of heaven and hell, will *have* to look for a saviour and a way of salvation before they can get their minds quiet again—and it's clear they won't get that from priests—and who knows but they may be driv to the Bible for that."

"Well, Jem," said Pat, "I think you are right; sure enough, it's new work the priests are at in preaching that way, and more may come of it than they know of.   If they stir the people to think in earnest about sin and their own souls, they'll maybe find they have riz what they cannot quell, for they haven't got what will satisfy them that are once in earnest about their own souls; and the Rev. Mr. Burke seemed to think that, too, for he kept writing mighty good letters to the people, showing them where they would find salvation and the way of peace with God, if they want to look for it now."

"But look here, Pat," said Jem; "see, here's a verse out of the Bible, stuck on to the end of the priest's paper; sure that's new anyway." So Jem read the verse—"Whosoever shall follow this rule, peace on them and mercy"—Galatians, ch. vi., ver. 16.

"And what rule was that about," said Pat;

"could it be about praying to the Blessed Virgin and looking to her for salvation, the way it is in this paper?"

So Pat got his Douay Bible, and he read— "God forbid that I should glory, save in the cross of our Lord Jesus Christ; by whom the world is crucified to me and I to the world. For in Jesus Christ neither circumcision availeth anything, nor uncircumcision, but a new creature. *And whosoever shall follow this rule, peace on them and mercy.*"—Galatians ch. vi., v. 14, 15, 16.

"Now, Pat," said Jem, "see what the rule in the Douay Bible is, *to glory in the cross of Jesus Christ, and nothing else*, and the promise of peace and mercy is to them that follow *that rule*. And now see if this paper isn't telling every one to pray to the Blessed Virgin and to look *to her* for salvation, without one word about Christ, the Saviour of sinners; and then they clap on to this rule of their own making the very promise that the Bible makes to them that look to Christ only. Now isn't that nothing else but turning the word and promise of God himself into a lie?"

"Jem," said Pat, "there's nothing else to be

got of our priests. They haven't the Gospel, and so they won't let us have the Bible ; and if we want the Gospel of Jesus Christ we must have the Bible for ourselves to teach us."

We print here the paper which the missionary priests printed and circulated about their mission, that our readers may see for themselves whether what Pat and Jem said about it was fair and true.

✠

JESUS, MARY, AND JOSEPH.

RESOLUTIONS AT THE CLOSE OF THE MISSION.

1st. Every day, either at morning or night prayers, I shall repeat and consider these great truths : GOD SEES ME, and *beholds even the secrets of my heart. I must die, and it may be this very day. After death I must be judged, and woe to me if I be found guilty of mortal sin, not repented of. Then begins Eternity, which I must spend amidst the joys of Heaven or torments of Hell.*

2ndly. Every day I shall be exact in saying my morning and night prayers ; I shall examine my conscience, I shall repeat the Angelus, say grace before and after meals, read a portion of a pious book (were it only for five or ten minutes), or recite a part of the Rosary of the Blessed Virgin.

3rdly. Every Sunday I shall assist devoutly at Mass, and, if possible, at a Sermon, and I shall read a *considerable portion* of a pious book ; I shall also consider the faults of the past week, and resolve to avoid them this week. Moreover, I shall examine how I have kept these resolutions, and I shall repeat them anew.

4thly. Every month, at least, I shall approach the Holy Sacraments of *Penance* and the *Blessed Eucharist.* But if I should have the misfortune of falling into mortal sin, I shall overcome every inconvenience in order to go to confession as *soon as possible,* knowing that *a person in mortal sin is liable at any moment to everlasting damnation.*

5thly. I shall avoid most carefully *every person, every place, and every thing* that would bring me into sin, but, above all, *such persons, such places, and such things* as have already led me into sin.

6thly. I shall make every effort, with the grace of God, to overcome *that temptation* which I know by experience to be most dangerous to me.

7thly. Every night I shall repeat the following prayer, to obtain, through the intercession of the Blessed Virgin, the grace of persevering in these resolutions until death :—

PRAYER OF ST. BERNARD.

Remember, O most pious Virgin, that it was never heard of in any age that those who implored and had recourse to thy powerful protection were ever abandoned by thee. I, therefore, O sacred Virgin, animated with the most lively confidence, cast myself at thy sacred feet, most earnestly and fervently beseeching thee to adopt me, though a wretched sinner, for thy perpetual child, to take care of my eternal salvation, and to watch over me at the hour of my death. O do not, mother of the Word Incarnate, despise my prayers, but graciously hear and obtain the grant of my petitions. Amen.

———

PRAYER OF THE MIRACULOUS MEDAL.

O MARY, conceived without sin, pray for us who have recourse to thee.

———

SPECIAL RECOMMENDATIONS.

TO THE PARISHIONERS AT LARGE.—Exact attendance at the public service of religion in the Church, zeal for the becoming style and decoration of the Church, as also for the vestments and other requisites of the altar, respect for the Clergymen, and submission to their advice.

To THE HEADS OF FAMILIES.—Instruction, vigilance, correction, and, above all, good example—prayer in common, proper choice of servants, attention to their religious duties.

To HUSBANDS AND WIVES.—Affection, mutual forbearance, union, and peace—send your children to good schools.

To CHILDREN.—Love, respect, and obedience to parents—peace and concord amongst themselves.

To MEN.—A horror of blaspheming, cursing, swearing, gambling, impure conversation, bad company, drunkenness, and public-houses, a love of honesty, the pardon of injuries.

To WOMEN.—Meekness, patience, charity, and attention to the duties of the house.

To YOUNG PEOPLE IN GENERAL.—To avoid dangerous occasions, wakes, dances, company-keeping, and bad books.

To YOUNG BOYS.—To avoid dangerous amusements, dread of everything contrary to modesty, to practise pious reading.

To YOUNG FEMALES.—Modesty, becomingness in dress, humility, particular devotion to the Blessed Virgin, the study and imitation of her virtues.

To ALL.—A spirit of piety, watchfulness, great distrust in ourselves, and unbounded confidence in God.

"Whosoever shall follow this rule, peace on them and mercy."—GAL. vi. 16.

Whether the prayer in the above paper was really written by St. Bernard, who lived in the 12th century, we do not know ; nor perhaps does it much signify.　But we do think it very strange that any prayer of St. Bernard should be put along with the prayer of the miraculous medal. "O Mary, CONCEIVED WITHOUT SIN, pray for us, who have recourse to thee;" for this reason, that St. Bernard condemned the notion of Mary being *conceived without sin*, as a FALSE DOCTRINE. If our readers will look to an article in the Catholic Layman, vol. iii., p. 97, they will find that St. Bernard affirms that this doctrine is "neither supported by reason nor backed by any tradition;" he says it was founded on "an alleged revelation which is destitute of adequate authority." He asks, "How can it be maintained that a conception which did not proceed from the Holy Ghost—not to say that it proceeded from sin—can be holy? or how could they conjure up a holy day on account of *a thing that is not holy in itself;*" and he says that the Feast of the Immaculate Conception (which is now celebrated in the Church of Rome) "either *honours sin* or *authorizes a false holiness.*"

All this St. Bernard wrote; yet the Roman Catholic priests do not scruple to put St. Bernard's name side by side with a prayer, "O, Mary, conceived without sin!"

Thus the priests deal with the Fathers; thus they reverence the opinions and authority of the

Fathers; but how could we expect them to deal more truly with the Fathers than they do with Scripture itself?

———

CHAPTER XXV.

THE FIRE OF PURGATORY.

"PAT, I have got something new to talk about," said Jem, pulling a roll of paper out of his pocket.

"Let us see it, Jem," said Pat. So Jem unrolled the paper, and showed a beautiful picture, with fine, bright colours in it.

So said Pat, "What is it at all, Jem?"

"Don't you see for yourself, Pat?" said Jem.

"Why, then, if it isn't the souls in Purgatory!" said Pat.

"'Deed and it isn't then; you're out for this time," said Jem; "so look again, Pat."

So Pat looked again; "And what else can you make of it at all?" said Pat.

"The *bodies* in purgatory," said Jem.

"Well, sure enough it is," said Pat; "sure enough them's bodies; them can't be souls, anyway. But isn't it mostly *souls* that goes to Purgatory?" said Pat, a little puzzled.

"Well, I never heard tell of any but souls going there, if so be they go there at all," said Jem ; "but you see yourself it's bodies that is in it."

"Sure enough it is, Jem," said Pat ; "and my ! but they're the purty creatures, them women, just like real ladies ! I wonder what they done at all to bring them there ? Would they be bad women, now ?" said Pat.

"Well, you know, Pat," said Jem, "that couldn't be ; for doesn't the catechism say that them that dies in mortal sin goes to hell for all eternity, and not to Purgatory ?"

"Aye," said Pat ; "but doesn't the catechism say, too, that them that gets their mortal sin, and the guilt of it, forgiven in this world, has still to go to Purgatory, for a time, to get the stains washed out of them before they can go to Heaven, where nothing defiled can enter ? and mightn't it be that way they got there ?"

"Well, maybe so," said Jem, "if so be that them that's forgiven goes there at all. But, when Jesus Christ said to the woman that was a sinner, *thy sins are forgiven ; thee* and when He allowed her to wash his feet with her tears, and wipe them with the hair of her head, and, more than all, when He finished with her by saying, *thy faith hath saved thee,* GO IN PEACE, did He just mean to bid her go to Purgatory ? or was that the meaning she took out of it ?"

" Well, Jem," said Pat, " I'm thinking if Jesus Christ had just took and shown her that picture, she wouldn't have *gone in peace* anyway."

" I'm thinking so, too," said Jem ; " and that when the Blessed Lord said them blessed words to the woman that was a sinner, He didn't mean the picture at all; and it's hard to think that them that's forgiven by Him will ever come to the like of what's in that picture."

" Well, if they was ever so bad," said Pat, " sure it would be only commonly decent, with their purty white skins, and the beautiful hair flowing down on their backs, to put a bit of a shift on them itself when their pictures was going to be took in Purgatory."

" Man alive," said Jem, " what good would that be ? Sure, look at the long flames just curling up all round them, and wouldn't the shift be burned off them afore you could look round ?"

" Well, I don't know for that," said Pat ; " sure there isn't so much as the sign of a scorch

* St. Luke, vii. 37, to the end.

on their beautiful skins ; and why couldn't the shift stand it as well ? Don't you mind in the Book of Daniel, when the wicked king put the three men in the fire, because they would not worship the golden image, the fire couldn't hurt their clothes no more than themselves."*

" Well, sure enough," said Jem, " the picture looks a deal more like people that the fire couldn't hurt at all than like people it could hurt ; and that being the way, they might as well have their clothes on, and I'm thinking it might be better too, in the picture ; for you know yourself, Pat, there's many a young boy that cares little for Purgatory that would buy that picture just for the bad thoughts that could be took out of it."

" Well, there's some in the picture dressed fine enough, anyway," said Pat ; " who would they be now ?"

" Sure, them's the angels taking the souls out of Purgatory," said Jem ; " don't you see the wings on them ?"

" Well, that's the elegant dress on that angel,"

* This history is in the fourth chapter of the Book of Daniel. N.B.—Observe, from verse 25 to verse 90 of this chapter in the Douay Bible, is *not* in Hebrew Bible—Daniel wrote in Hebrew : neither is it in the Protestant Bible ; but the account of the men being saved in the fire is in both Bibles.

said Pat; "that's the beautiful green bedgown, and the purtiest red petticoat ever I seen. Sure the finest lass at a fair would be proud to be an angel, to wear such a bedgown and petticoat!"

"'Deed and she might," said Jem; "but sure a girl that wore the like of that would, at least, have the shoes on her arm going to a fair or a market."

"But what's this, at all, at the top," said Pat, "with all the bright light about it? Well, it's the cross and a lamb on it. Won't that be Jesus now?"

"That's what it's meant for," said Jem; "the Lamb of God that taketh away the sins of the world;* and don't you see the blood running from its throat, and the angels catching the blood in golden cups, and pouring it out on the people in Purgatory?"

"And is it the blood of Christ and not the fire, after all, that cleanses them that's in Purgatory?" said Pat; "and is it only *waiting* in the fire they are till they get the blood of Christ? didn't I think that sins were forgiven in this life by the blood of Christ, and that them that was forgiven had to go to Purgatory to get their stains

* Gospel of St. John i. 29.

bleached out of their souls by the fire itself? but if it's the blood of Christ that cleanses too, what is the fire for at all?"

"Well, it's just for to punish them," said Jem.

"Don't tell me of *punishment* for them that's *forgiven*," said Pat; "that's not reason, and it's not gospel. Either the fire is to cleanse out the stains of the soul, after the sins is forgiven, or it's for nothing at all; and *which* does the cleansing, is it the blood of Christ, or is it the fire?"

"Well, Pat," said Jem; "the Bible tells us of forgiveness of sins through the blood of Christ; and it tells us just the same of the *cleansing* too. Sure, doesn't it say—'How much more shall the blood of Christ, who by the Holy Ghost offered Himself unspotted unto God, CLEANSE our conscience from dead works, to serve the living God.'* And if the blood of Christ does *all*, what is the fire for?"

"Well, Jem," said Pat, "here's the differ of the Bible and the picture. *Both* allows that the blood of Christ does it; but, by the Bible the blood of Christ does it *now;* and by the picture,

* Hebrews, ix. 14 (Douay Bible).

the blood of Christ won't cleanse us till we get to Purgatory."

"Well, I think that's it," said Jem. "Sure we have the Bible and the picture to choose between."

"Well, thank God for having the choice anyway," said Pat. "Which, I wonder, would the priests like us to follow?"

"Well, Pat," said Jem, "I got this picture in a shop that had plenty more, just nigh hand to the great Carmelite Church in York-row, in Dublin. Sure the priests like to see it set up in the windows; if they don't like it, why don't they stop it? Sure it isn't Protestants sells that! And why don't they say a word against it? Why don't they warn the people against it, the way they do against reading the Bible? Sure the priests like the picture well, and why wouldn't they give it to us for our religion. I'm thinking there is a deal of things in our religion would be better took off it, if any priest would only set about it."

"Well, Jem," said Pat, "I thought that last week, when I seen Peter M'Kenna buying a horse in Kilcommon fair; and the horse had a big bush of a tail on him, and Peter got him cheap, for he ran him down for falling away entirely in the hind quarters ; and when Peter got him into a yard, he just backed him up to the wrong end of a cart, and whipped the big tail off him, and then he stood a one-side, and says Peter—' Now, isn't that a great addition to him entirely ?'   And thinks I to myself, wouldn't it be a great addition to our religion if it was well docked too."

" Well, never mind the horse, Pat," said Jem. " But sure enough there's a deal to come off our religion, and the more the Bible gets out, the sooner it will be done."

And the more we hear of the talk of plain people, like Pat and Jem, the more hope we have that the Bible will get out indeed.

CHAPTER XXVI.

PASTORS AND FLOCKS.

" THEM's hard times, Jem," said Pat.

" That's true anyway, Pat," said Jem; "it's not easy keeping the meal to the children these times. But sure we have a right to be thankful it's no worse."

" Well, Jem," said Pat, " I heard Mr. Nulty talking of that, and he allowed that if the crops was short this year, it's the famine we would have back again; so we have a right to be thankful sure enough."

" And it's the poor thing, too, that the Rooshians, with their fighting, should stint the childer of the meal," said Jem. " I wonder will it be soon over."

" Well, I heard Mr. Nulty allow it wouldn't," said Pat; "and he allowed there would be mighty heavy taxes on the farmers and the gentlemen to pay for it; so you see all gets their pinch by it as well as we."

" Well, it's not bad times yet with the farmers," said Jem; " they're pretty snug for a while anyway. But I suppose they will get their turn of the pinch too."

"Well, most all comes in for it by turns," said Pat; "but there's some getting the pinch sore enough these years back that there isn't much said of."

"And who would that be ?" said Jem.

"Why it's the priests, Jem," said Pat; " sure it's they got the pinch in earnest in the famine times, and hasn't come round yet like the farmers."

"Well," said Jem, "I don't think times is hard on Father John, and sure there's Father Peter, the curate, and Father Brady, of the next parish, and enough more of them, that keeps their hunters as fine as ever."

"Well, there's some of them not much the worse," said Pat; "but even Father John hasn't near what he had ; and there's a deal of the priests that got it sore in the famine times, and that isn't much better yet ; you see, Jem, where the farms is good, and the farmers strong, the priest gets his share now as well as ever ; but where the priests were depending to the little man, it went to the bad with them entirely. Sure the poor people can't pay them now the way they used ; and there isn't the marrying and the christening there used to be ; and there's a deal of places where the poor people itself isn't in it ;

and what can the priest do there? and where there's large Protestant grazing farms, and the poor people's houses down, sure the priests may go starve."

"Well, it's the poor thing, sure enough," said Jem, "for them that was bred to be clargy, and had such a rule in the country, to come to that. Sure they can't do without it no more nor ourselves, and they're not used to it; and it doesn't come natural to clargy, the way it does to the like of us. Sure I would be sorry for Father John himself, if he was at a dis-short; but it makes again them greatly when some of them keeps their hunters, and goes a skevying across the country, after the hounds; 'deed, I thought many a time it would be no worse for them if they would take after the Protestant clergy in that. But what becomes of them at all where they gets nothing?"

"Well, I heard a deal about that, when I was down at the fairs in Connaught," said Pat. "I was talking to the men that driv up the cattle from the out-of-the-way plases, and they allowed there wasn't half the priests in it there used to be; and them that was there had little enough to live on, and maybe it's getting less was the little."

" And where are the priests that's not in it?" said Jem.

" Why, there's some in America, and some in Australia," said Pat.

" Well, sure if they follow the people, won't they do as well as ever?" said Jem.

" They won't, Jem," said Pat ; " by all accounts the people isn't the same in America as they is here. Don't you mind Father Mullen's letter that we read in the newspaper,* that made it out that two millions of the Irish had turned in America. Sure it isn't them the priests can live by. You see, Jem, America is a kind of a place where every man does what he likes."

" Well, I wonder why people doesn't do what they like in Ireland, as well as in America," said Jem ; " but, sure enough, they don't ; what's the reason at all ?"

" Well, I had a talk about that with a man that drove up the sheep that Mr. Nulty bought at Ballinasloe," said Pat ; " he was a mighty cute sensible man ; and we fell into talk, and I asked him that very same ; and says he, ' do you mind them sheep,' says he ; ' now, while you keep them

* See extracts from this letter in the *Catholic Layman* for September, 1862, vol. L, p. 103.

together on the road, where the one goes they'll all go,' says he, 'and you'll just have no trouble at all ; but, if you wonst let them get one in one field, and another in another field, why, then, every sheep goes after its own nose, and no two goes the same way ; and it's the more they'll scatter,' says he, 'and the harder on you to gather them ; and that's the way with men too,' says he ; 'keep them together, and they'll go the one way ; but, once they scatter, then every man goes the way he likes, and no man thinks no more about what every body does ; so you mind the sheep and keep them all together,' says he."

"And will the Irish people go the one way for ever in Ireland, without minding the way they would like to go ?" said Jem.

"Why, man alive," said Pat, "don't you see yourself, if a bully of a sheep just makes a bolt at the hedge, all the rest goes bolt after him too ; and sure it's in the field they will be in spite of you. Sure it's in the field they would all like to be ; and, when the bully goes, won't they be after him ?"

"Aye," said Jem, "I see that surely ; but where will we get the right sort of bully in Ireland ? Sure it's sheep we are, but there isn't the bullies in it."

So Pat looked Jem right hard in the face, as if he was going to be the bully to make the bolt himself—only he wasn't. "So," said Pat, looking as hard as he could, "Jem, it's a right bully of a priest I would like to see, of the right sort ; and wouldn't *he* have the following ?"

"And what would you have him to do, at all ?" said Jem.

So Pat looked harder at Jem than ever ; and he said, with a fire that seemed to be dancing in his eye, "Jem, as I'm a living man, there's a something afore us in Ireland ; and a PRIEST, with THE BIBLE in his hand, is what Ireland wants."

"And would you have him to turn, and have the bishop on his back ?" said Jem.

"I don't want him to turn neither backward nor forward," said Pat, "but to hold up the Douay Bible in his hand, and to call on the Irish people ; that's the man that Ireland's waiting for, and that's the man for the following ; and it isn't the bishop on his back he need think about, for it's Ireland he will have at his back."

"And would he be a Protestant all out, Pat?" said Jem.

"Well, that isn't so easy seen, Jem," said Pat. "You see if a man quits the Mass and goes to Church, he changes his name plain enough; but, if a priest only stands up in the chapel, and holds up a Douay Bible in his hand and says, 'Boys, it's the Word of God that is able to save our souls,' it isn't so easy seen if that makes them all Protestants. Anyway, it's not as plain as a man walking, by himself alone, out of the chapel into the church."

"Aye, but where would that stop, Pat?" said Jem.

"It wouldn't stop short of the Word of God, Jem," said Pat; "and why should it; and who could say again it? Who *could* stop it, at all? Neither crook nor crozier, if that bolt was made by the right bully. Wouldn't all Ireland turn round to the priest with the Bible in his hand?"

"And will the like of that ever be, Pat?" said Jem.

"Jem," said Pat, "there has been trouble from God in Ireland. His hand done it. There was trouble on the people, and trouble on the priest. And it's not for nothing. The hearts of the people is stirred, like what they never was before; and there seems to be something that the hearts of the people wants; and it can't be nothing but the Word that comes from God. There's a something afore us; and it's THE MAN we're waiting on."

Time will tell if Pat has rightly comprehended the feeling of poor men like himself. And, perhaps, "the man," when he comes, may look back to the words of Pat.

CHAPTER XXVII.

THE OLD COAT.

PAT and Jem did not get together for a good while to have a talk; but at last they fell in on the road, and were walking together; but Pat did little at the talking, but kept looking mighty hard at his old coat, first at one sleeve and then at the other, and then on the big patches on the breast of it.

And, indeed, poor Pat's coat was very bad. It was once made all of blue frieze, and then it must have looked very smart; but, when times got hard, Pat had to get a piece on the coat betimes, because he never had the price of a new one; so there were brown patches, and grey patches, and patches the colour of mud; and there were the legs of two old stockings, sewed over the arms, from the wrists to the elbows, to keep the patches together; and all the patches looked as if the best wife in the country could not keep them together much longer.

So Pat kept looking mighty hard at his coat, and talking little.

"What's the matter with the coat at all?" said Jem.

"Well, I'm studying the old coat," said Pat.

"Is it how to get a new one you mean?" said Jem.

"Time enough to study that when the meal gets cheaper," said Pat; "it's this *old* coat I'm studying."

"Well, and what do you make out of the old one?" said Jem.

"Well, I had a discussion on it last night," said Pat, "and I didn't think there was as much to be got out of an old coat."

"And what's to be got out of it?" said Jem; "tell us that, Pat."

"Well," said Pat, "I was in last night at old

Ned Flanagan's, and there was a deal of people in it, and there was Tim Reilly, the priest's schoolmaster; and they were all talking about the old religion and the new religion; and Tim Reilly was holding out that the Church of Rome had the old religion; and others was asking wasn't there things changed in it, and then how could it be the old religion? and at first Tim Reilly wouldn't give in that there was anything changed; but there was old Ned Flanagan, that gets a newspaper, called the CATHOLIC LAYMAN, and he had a deal of learning out of it; and, indeed, he promised me the reading when he had done with it. So, says he to Tim, 'Is the Immaculate Conception an article of the Catholic faith?' says he. 'It is,' said Tim; 'didn't you hear the priest read the Pope's decree in the chapel?' 'And how could St. Bernard be a saint when he denied it?' said Ned. 'It wasn't an article of the faith then,' said Tim, 'for the Pope hadn't settled it.' 'Well,' says I, 'sure that's a new piece put on it anyway; and how can it be the old religion after that?'

"Well, with that he turns rounds to me; for he's a mighty cute little fellow, that would bother anybody; and says he, 'how long have you the old coat ?' says he. 'It's turning the talk, you are,' says I. 'It's not,' says he; 'it's coming to it I am : how long have you the old coat ?' says he again. Well, they all allowed me to answer him: so, says I, 'It's eight years anyway, and may be a bit more.' 'And mighty well mended it is,' says he, 'for the time. Now, do you mean to tell me,' says he, 'that you bought that coat eight years ago ?' says he. ''Deed and I do,' says I. 'That very coat ?' says he. 'This very coat,' says I. So he puts his hand on my shoulder, and, says he, 'Was this patch on when you got it ?' says he. 'No,' says I. 'Nor none of the patches ?' says he. 'Not one of them,' says I. 'And it's the same coat for all that,' says he.

"Well, I seen then what he was at ; and when I came to think of it, it wasn't easy to think it *was* the same coat, when there was hardly a bit of the first coat left in it. 'Well, I think it's hardly the same, after all,' says I. 'Well, boys,' says he, 'did you ever hear the like of that ? Didn't he say this minute it was the very coat ?'

"Well, they were all down on me then ; and I tried to make the best hand I could of it; 'for sure,' says I, 'it isn't like it, for it was a blue coat when I got it, and I leave it to yourselves, boys,

if you can find one bit of the blue cloth in it now.'
Well, with that the boys all began discussing if
it was the same coat or not ; and some allowed
that as long as I took it off at night, and put it
on in the morning, it was surely the same coat ;
and more of them allowed it was the cloth that
made the coat ; and when the same cloth wasn't
in it, how could it be the same coat. Well,
when they were all done talking, says Tim to me
—'Is it the same coat,' says he, ' or is it not ?'
' Well, I think it's not,' says I. 'And *when* did
it turn into another coat ?' says he ; 'was it when
the first patch was put on it ?' says he. 'No,'
says I, 'it wasn't, sure enough.' 'And was it
the second patch, or the third patch, or the
fourth patch, or what patch,' says he, ' that
turned it into another coat ?' says he. Well,
with that they all began again, and now they
were all for allowing that it *was* the same coat.
Well, Ned Flanagan's byre is down, and so he
had the cow in the corner. So I turns to Ned,
and says I, ' That's a pretty little calf,' says I.
' It's no calf,' said Ned, ' it's a cow giving milk
with a calf of her own.' 'Don't be joking,' says
I, 'it's a calf.' 'It's joking you are,' says he.
' Was it ever a calf,' says I. ' It was,' says he.

'What day did it turn into a cow?' says I; 'was it a Sunday or a week-day? Here's a learned man,' says I, pointing to Tim, 'that will prove to you that it's a calf still, if you can't tell the day it changed.' Well, with that they all allowed the day couldn't be told, and still the calf had turned into a cow.

"'And,' says I, 'isn't it the same with the corn that grows—*who* can tell the day the ear is formed? and isn't it the way with spring and summer? and with child and man? and isn't it the way with day and night? and where's the good,' says I, 'of the priest telling us our religion must be the same now that it was at first, just because no one can tell what day it changed from one religion to another; and wouldn't just the same argument prove,' says I, 'that night was day, or day night? But who would be the fool to believe it against his own eyesight?' says I, 'and where's the good of argument that's as fit to prove that black is white as to prove anything else?' says I.

"Well, with that they all fell to talking, and they allowed that things does change, in a way that no one can tell *when* they changed, and that there is no use denying it.

"Well, I was considering with myself that when a thing is said sharp and clever about one thing being like another, people, maybe, is apt to take it up mighty quick, and think it very learned, without stopping to consider how far one thing *is* like another; so, thinks I to myself, '*would* the religion of Jesus Christ be like an old coat at all?

"So I turns to Tim Reilly, and, says I, 'After all, there's a differ between the coat getting old and the calf turning into a cow, and I give in to you entirely that it's the very same coat I bought eight years ago.'

"'To be sure there's a differ,' says he, 'between a thing getting old and one thing turning into another, and that's what I was going to say when you would be done talking,' says he; so then, he went on to talk a deal about the old coat being the same, with all its patches; and just the same way, he allowed, when the Pope made new decrees and new articles of faith, his religion was still the same religion, and the old religion for all that.

"So I waited till he was done; and then says I, 'And do you mean to tell me,' says I, 'that the religion of Jesus Christ is made up of patches and mendings, like an old coat. You're right so far anyway,' says I, 'that your religion is old enough, like the old coat,' says I; 'it's as old as being patched and mended, and thread-bare, and darned, and in rags and holes, and tossed and turned, can make it; but you'll never get the holes out of an old coat by turning it,' says I; 'and isn't it enough for me to have my old coat made of rags and patches without having my religion made of them too?' says I; 'and isn't that the way with all them that tries to patch up a religion of their own merits, instead of the merits of Christ; for doesn't the Bible say that "all our righteousnesses are as filthy rags"?* And *why* do I patch the old coat?' says I. 'Isn't it because it's wearing out? and when it's patched it's changed for the worse any way from what it was once. And can that be the way with the religion that God made? Doesn't the Bible say that the heavens and the earth will wear out like an old coat, but that God keeps still the self-same ever more?† And

* Isaiah lxiv. 6, and compare Romans x. 3.

† Thou in the beginning, O Lord, didst found the earth : and the works of thy hands are the heavens.

They shall perish, but Thou shalt continue : and they shall all grow old as a garment.

And as a vesture shalt Thou change them : and they shall be changed : but Thou art the self-same, and thy years shall not fail.—Hebrews i. 10, 11, 12, and Psalm ci. 26, 27, 28, Douay Bible; Psalm cii. 25, 26, 27 in the Protestant Bible.

T

won't his religion keep the same ? " for the word of the Lord endureth for ever ;"* so I leave you the old coat for your religion,' says I ; 'but it won't fit the religion of Christ ; for there never was a coat,' says I, 'but *the one*, that could be fitting for the religion of Christ.'

" Well, with that they all began tearing at me to tell what coat that was ; and I made them guess for it, and of all the guesses ever you heard they were the quarest ; one allowed it was what the priest says mass in ; another said it was what the nuns wear on their heads ; another said it was the red strip that some of the priests wear over their shoulder ; one old woman said it be to be the scapular ; another said it was the blue cloak that's on the picture of the Virgin Mary in the chapel ; and another allowed that it be to be something that was on the Pope : but they could make no hand of it, till old Ned Flanagan, that reads his Bible, says, 'Why, then, wasn't it the coat of Christ himself, that was " without seam, woven from the top throughout." '† 'That's the hit,' says I ; 'would there be seams and patches iu the religion of Christ, any more than on his coat ?' So with that, for it was getting late, says I to Tim Reilly,

* 1 Peter L 25, Douay Bible.   † Gospel of St. John xix. 23.

'I'll just take myself off with my old coat,' says I; 'and may you get the religion without seams. or patches, afore I get a new coat.' So they bid me good night kindly, and maybe they will think of the coat."

"Well, Pat," said Jem, "you done it well : and 'deed I didn't know there was so much good to be got in an old coat ; and when times mend, and you get a new one, I hope it will serve you as well."

We hope so, too, and we hope the state of poor Pat's coat will remind some rich people how much the poor want some warm clothing in this cold weather, when the most a poor man's wages. can do is to get a little meal at a dear price, and maybe little enough of that. May God stir up the hearts of us all to remember how "the religion without seam" teaches us to feed the hungry and to clothe the naked.

CHAPTER XXVIII.

CONFESSION.

"Well, Pat," said Jem, when they met last, "is there anything new to talk of ?"

"I don't know about its being new, Jem," said

Pat : " maybe it's not old enough ; but it's an old thing with me, anyway."

" And what is it ?" said Jem.

" It's confession, Jem," said Pat.

" And were you at confession, Pat ?" said Jem.

" No, Jem," said Pat, " I wasn't. It's long enough since I was there."

" And was it reading the Bible put you off it, Pat ?" said Jem.

" No, Jem, it wasn't that put me off it," said Pat : " sure, I quit confession, like a deal of the boys, long afore ever I took to reading ; so, it wasn't that."

" Well, there's a deal of the boys, surely, that doesn't read the Bible, nor go to confession either," said Jem ; " more maybe than does go, a great deal. And I'm thinking they're getting more and more ; and what's the reason, if it's not the reading that does it ?"

" Well, the times done a deal of it, Jem," said Pat. " Sure, it was the famine put me off it ; for I hadn't the dust to pay. Not but what the priest would hear my confession if I hadn't the money ; but, then, you know, Jem, they don't like not to see the money ; and people doesn't like to go without the money ; and that put me off it first."

"Well but, Pat," said Jem, "the times got better, and sure you might get the shilling then ?"

"Aye, I could," said Pat ; "but, then, how would I remember all the sins I committed in five years maybe?   And if I couldn't mind them, how would I confess them ?   And then where was the use of going ?   So, one way or another, I quit confession long afore I took to the reading."

"'Deed, Pat," said Jem, " there's a deal, I believe, quit it just in the same way.   But, are you going to take to it again now ?"

"Not till I find it in the Bible, Jem," said Pat.

"And what set you talking about it, then ?" said Jem.

"The wife, Biddy, set me talking about it," said Pat. "Sure, she was at confession, and she wouldn't quit talking about it, wanting me to go, too."

"And what did you say to her ?" said Jem.

"'Won't I confess my sins to God,' says I ; 'and won't He be faithful and just to forgive me my sins ?'* says I.

* 1st Epistle of St. John i. 9.

"'And what good will that do you,' says she, 'if you don't get absolution from the priest?'

"'And do you mean,' says I, 'that if God forgives me, the priest can send me to hell?' says I.

"'But how will you know it,' says she, 'if the priest doesn't say it?'

"'Well,' says I, 'I suppose that's the good of confession and absolution, just to make it more sure when we hear the priest say it.'

"'To be sure it is,' says she; 'sure *then* we're sure we are forgiven, when we hear it said; and how would we know it without?'

"'And mustn't we make a good confession, Biddy, dear?' says I.

"'To be sure we must,' says she; 'it's no good without that.'

"'Then the priest saying the absolution over me,' says I, 'is just no security at all to me, only as far as I can be sure that I made a good confession?' says I.

"'Well,' says she, 'sure it's the easiest thing in life to make a good confession to the priest; sure, if you do what pleases him, he won't be hard on you at all.'

"'Well, Biddy,' says I, 'it be to be a good confession, or it's no absolution after all; and if the priest lets me off a good confession, sure he is only letting me off the absolution.'

" 'It's the easiest thing in life,' says she, 'to make a good confession to the priest.'

" 'And isn't it just as easy,' says I, 'to make the same confession to God ? But Biddy, dear,' says I, ' what have you to confess to the priest ?'

" 'All my mortal sins,' says she.

" 'Since when ?' says I.

" 'Since I went to confession afore,' says she.

" 'How long is that ?' says I.

" 'This time twelvemonth,' says she.

" 'And did you mind all your deadly sins since that ?' says I.

" 'Why wouldn't I ?' says she ; 'sure they're not that many.'

" 'And how long did it take you ?' says I.

" 'Not the turn of my hand,' says she ; 'for his reverence was in a hurry, and a deal of people waiting.'

" 'Maybe some was forgot in the hurry,' says I. 'Tell me, Biddy, dear,' says I, 'isn't anger one of the seven deadly sins ?'

" 'It is,' says she.

" 'And did you tell him every time you were

angry at me and the childer, for the last year?'
says I.

"'How would I?' says she, 'when the childer
angers me every turn of the day, and it's forgot
as soon as over,' says she.

"'And was that confessing all your mortal
sins for the year, Biddy?' says I.

"'And what can I do?' says she. 'Sure, I
can't go to confession every day in the year,' says
she.

"''Deed can you, Biddy,' says I.

"'Is it nonsense you're talking?' says she ;
'where would I get time, or where would I get
priests enough, or where would I get all the
shillings?' says she. 'Sure it would take a
man's wages,' says she.

"'I'll show you the way, Biddy, dear,' says I.
'If we take to confessing our sins to God, sure
it's every night we will do that, Biddy ; and we
can tell them to Him while they're on our minds,
and ask His pardon, and ask Him, too, to help
us the next day; and won't that keep us watching
ourselves? But when we leave it for once a-year
to the priest, why, the sins are all forgot, and
then they're not confessed at all, and then there's

no absolution, nor nothing to keep us watching every day. That's the reason,' says I, ' that I would rather confess my sins to God, because it makes a better confession,' says I.

" ' And didn't Jesus Christ command us to confess our sins to the priest,' says she ; ' and how will it be if we don't ?'

" ' Can you say the Ten Commandments of God, Biddy ?' says I.

" ' To be sure I can,' says she ; ' aren't they in our catechism ?'

" ' Is confession among them ?' says I.

" ' No, then, it's not,' says she.

" ' And what commandments is it in ?' says I.

' " It's in the commandment of the Church,' says she. ' Sure enough, that's the way it is in the catechism.'

" ' Well, Biddy,' says I, ' isn't it all nonsense for them to be telling us that Jesus Christ commanded it Himself, when their own catechisms allow that it is only a commandment of the Church ? Sure, if He commanded it, wouldn't it be in the commandments of God ?'

" ' And who commanded it on us, then,' says she, ' if Jesus Christ did not ?'

" ' The priests *did*, and Jesus Christ *didn't*,'

says I. 'Sure, that's just the meaning of its being in the commandments of the Church, and not in the commandments of God.'

"'Well,' says she, 'anyway, I'd never be easy in my mind, if I didn't go to confession once a-year.'

"'Well, Biddy, dear,' says I, 'sure I'll never say again your going, as long as it is in your mind to go. But, sure, Biddy, dear,' says I, 'it wouldn't do any harm, anyway, to confess your sins to God, too.' So she allowed it wouldn't. 'And now, Biddy, dear,' says I, 'wouldn't we just lay it down for ourselves to go, both of us, on our knees to God every night, and confess our sins for that day, and ask His pardon, and ask Him to help us against them the next day; and, when Easter comes round again, you can go to the priest if you like; and then you'll be the better judge, Biddy,' says I, 'whether confessing to the priest once a-year, or confessing to God every night, makes the best confession,' says I. Well, so Biddy agreed to do the same, and we've both done it every night since. And now, you would wonder to see how Biddy tries not to be angered at the children. And, 'deed, Jem, since I put Biddy on that, it's making myself mighty careful, too, about things I thought little of before. And, maybe, when Easter comes round, Biddy will think that confessing to God makes the best confession."

"Well, 'deed, Pat," said Jem, "I think it's a good way you took, and the best way of all to learn what's best. Sure, it's a deal better than if you tried to stop Biddy going to the priest. And, 'deed, when a person tries that way, they'll find that it's not so easy to make a good confession to the priest once a-year. And, sure, if confession isn't done in reality, there's no good in absolution ; and how can a man know, at the end of a year, if he made a good confession at all ? and he getting, maybe, three minutes, more or less, to make it ?"

"Well, I think that's the great harm of it, Jem," said Pat ; "the people goes to the priest once a-year, and maybe not that often, and just says a few words to him in a hurry, and then thinks it's done, and all right ; and then never thinks more of it till next year ; and it's just the greatest stopper at all to people confessing their sins in real earnest. Sure, if a man goes to confess them to God every night, while he minds them himself and knows that God saw them, it will make him sore and sorry to have to tell the same sins every night, and make him pray the more for pardon and help, and make him strive more, too. But, when he goes once a-year to the priest, and gets clear of all in the turn of his hand, won't he just go on the same for the next year, and trust to get clean as easy? It's just like paying by Peter Burrowes,* so it is; and, sure, that never made a man honest or industrious."

"Well, 'deed, Pat," said Jem, "I thought that once myself when I got to the sea shore near Drogheda, after I had the sickness, and I met Peter Reilly, the blacksmith, that is working in a great factory in Drogheda now; and he's the hardest working boy at all, and the dirtiest boy at all; for his face is as black as a sweep with the coal-dust, and his clothes that dirty with the coals and the grease they use in the factory, that you wouldn't like to touch them with the end of a stick. And Peter had just come out of the sea, washed for once in his life, and had just got the clothes on him when I came up. 'And isn't it the pity,' says I, 'to see you in the dirty

---

* A saying in part of Ireland, for getting clear of a man's debts in the Insolvent Court, of which Mr. Burrowes was a judge.

clothes again, after the washing you got ?' 'Well, then,' says he, ' I'm as easy in the clothes now as if I had been confessing to the priest ; sure washing is like confessing,' says he ; ' it lasts the year, anyway.' "

"Aye, that's too like what the people thinks that confesses to the priest, and then thinks themselves all right to go on again just the way they did before," said Pat ; " but I'm trusting Biddy will think different afore Easter next."

And we trust that many of the Irish people may think different about confession of sins.

CHAPTER XXIX.

THE HOLY WELL AND THE RAGS.

" Jem, did you ever see a holy well ?" said Pat.

"Why wouldn't I, Pat ?" said Jem ; " sure there's enough of them, though they're not as plenty as they were when I was young ; but there's enough still ; and I seen them many a time, with the rags on the bushes, and the cut knees, and the whiskey, and the prayers, and the card-playing, and what not ? But why do you ask, Pat ?"

" Well," said Pat, " I was down in Galway to

fetch up some sheep, and I come iu for a pattern at a holy well, and it was a sight anyway ; of all the people ever you saw there was there ; and some crawling on their knees round the well, and some praying, and some drinking, and some courting ; and for the thorn bushes, you would take them to be patchwork quilts, with the sewing left out ; and I took to thinking what was it for at all ; so I goes up to an old creature that was cutting her knees creeping round the well, and, says I, 'What are you serving your old bones that way for ?' says I. 'Isn't it getting quit of my sins ?' says she. 'Well,' says I, ' sure I'm a Catholic long enough, and I never got quit of my sins that way, and never a priest ever told me of that way of getting quit of them.' 'Och, jewel,' says she, 'sure you're at the right place at last, and why don't you turn up the knees of your breeches and get quit of your sins ?' And now isn't that the quare way, Jem? and is it the Catholic religion at all ?"

" Well, Pat," said Jem, "it *is* the Catholic religion, or it *isn't.*   If it is, why did the priest never tell you that way to get quit of your sins ? and if it *isn't,* why does the priests allow them poor creatures to be deceiving their own souls with such folly?"

"Well, Jem," said Pat, "I learned something about that anyway; for I was stopping in a decent man's house, and, indeed, he was a very knowledgeable man, and he has a deal of old Irish books, and I fell to talking to him about the holy well; and, at first, he wouldn't let on that he knew anything about it; 'but,' says he, 'sure the people always did it;' but when he seen that I didn't think much of the well, he let out his mind; 'and sure,' says he, 'I have something about it here in a. book;' and he fetched down a book that was written by Dr. O'Connor, that was a priest, and, he said, was the learnedest priest that ever was in Ireland, and one of the real ould O'Connors of Ballynagare, that come of the kings of Ireland; and he showed me out of the book that Father O'Connor said the holy wells was all paganism; and how the heathens had the holy wells in Ireland in the time of St. Patrick and Columbkill, and how some stuck to it after, in spite of them, and how it was part of the worship of Baal, the god of the heathens, that the Israelites worshipped on Mount Carmel, in the time of Elijah.—1 Kings xviii. ; 3 Kings, Douay Bible. ' So,' says he, ' there's something old in our religion anyway ; for holy wells is older than the Christian religion itself, for they're as old as paganism ; so it's a fine religion, it is,' says he."

" And the rags, Pat," said Jem ; " where did they get them ?"

" Well, if he didn't show me that, too, out of Father O'Connor's book," said Pat ; " for I asked him, and he just turned to a page where Father O'Connor says, that some travellers were going through a heathen country, away beyond the Crimea, where the soldiers is, and they found a tree all covered over with rags, just the same as a bush beside a holy well, and it was people with the ague stuck them there to get cured ; so there's paganism again for you, Jem."

" I wonder why the Catholic Church lets people follow paganism instead of the Christian religion," said Jem.

" Well, I seen in Father O'Connor's book that the canons of the Church is against it," said Pat ; " and that the Catholic Church isn't to be blamed for it at all ; and he says a deal of the bishops would like to stop it."

"And why *don't* they stop it, then ?" said Jem.

"Well," said Pat, "I suppose it was because the people was so fond of the holy wells that they couldn't."

"Well, Pat," said Jem, "if the bishops wasn't able to stop paganism, isn't it enough to make a body guess that they weren't the right bishops at all ? But did any one ever hear tell of them trying ?"

"Well, Father O'Connor doesn't say they did," said Pat. "But he tells about Bishop Milner anyway ; that's the man that wrote a book called 'The End of Controversy,' that the priests get all their learning out of, against the Protestants."

"Aye, I seen that book with the priest's clerk," said Jem ; "but what about Bishop Milner ?"

"Why, Father O'Connor allows that Bishop Milner wrote a book crying up the holy well of St. Winifred, for the miraculous cures that it worked ; and, seemingly, Bishop Milner was mighty mad at Father O'Connor for saying what he did of holy wells," said Pat.

"And did Bishop Milner cry up the rags, too ?" said Jem.

U

"Well, I can't say for that," said Pat ; "for I didn't see that book ; but *there* is one bishop for you anyway that helped on the paganism, instead of stopping it."

"And did any ever try to stop it ?" said Jem.

"Well, that's just what I asked the man that showed me the book," said Pat ; says I, 'did any priest try to stop the people going to a holy well ?'

"''Deed did they,' says he ; 'I seen them do it a few years back.'

"'And *could* they do it ?' says I.

"'Quite easy,' says he, 'once they tried it in earnest.　The people just quit the well at once when the priest gave the orders.'

"'Well,' says I, 'there's some of the priests anyway that's for stopping paganism.'

"'Sorrow bit you'll say that,' says he, 'when you hear why they did it.　It's down the country a bit,' says he, 'and it was the greatest well at all, with rags enough on the bushes to cure all Ireland, if it was any good ; and there comes a clergyman out of Dublin, one Mr. Gregg, and he just takes a slip off a branch of the bush, with all the rags on it, and away he goes about England and Ireland with it in his hand, just to show people the Catholic religion ; and with that there comes lots of Englishmen just to look at the well and the bush ; and then the priests gave out that no one was to go to the well any more ; and there was an end of the holy well at wonst.' "

"I seen that same man and his twig," said Jem. "I was in Kilcommon one day, and I seen a great meeting, and I just went to it, and I seen him with the twig in a glass-case, and him holding it up, and it with the rags on it, and *that's* the man that *has* the Irish tongue ; now you couldn't help listening to him, like as if he was singing a song ; and he told how that twig built a church and a school-house, beside that same holy well ; and how the church is full of people that gets the water of life out of the Holy Scriptures now. So I don't wonder that the priests made the people quit *that* well ; for may-be them that went there would get *the living water once for all*, like the way the woman of Samaria got it at the well."—John iv. 10-15.

"So you see, Jem," said Pat, "the priests *can* stop the paganism, when the Protestants make them ashamed and afraid."

"Aye," said Jem, "the priests is following, not leading, when they put down the like of that. Why didn't they do it always? And why don't they do it everywhere now?"

"Well, Jem," said Pat, "sure it's getting plain every day that it's the Word of God, and not the priests, that will drive out the darkness and ignorance out of the people's minds, and let the true light shine in old Ireland. Will we ever see the paganism and the darkness put out, and the religion of Christ just what He made it Himself, and the people looking to the Saviour only to put away their sins?"

"Well," said Jem, "isn't it going on anyway? Isn't here two of us that has learned a deal these last two years; isn't there hope that a deal more may learn the same way?"

Those that have this hope, we trust will be stirred up to aid in promoting the enlightenment of the Irish people. Every one who learns to look at the True Light, is himself an instrument to show that Light to others.

If anyone should wish to see more of the book that was shown to Pat, he may find it in "Columbanus' Letters," written by Dr. Charles O'Connor, an Irish priest, of whose learning and talents Irishmen may justly be proud. The passage relating to holy wells is in the third letter, vol. i., pp. 73 to 105, and is well worthy of being read by anyone who wishes to understand what is practised in Ireland, and the origin of the practice. This letter was published in the year 1810, and very sorely Dr. O'Connor was handled for it by Bishop Milner and others. Dr. O'Connor speaks of Bishop Milner's "miraculous pamphlet" in defence of the well of St. Winifred. We have not seen that pamphlet, and should be much obliged to any of our readers who can tell us where it can be found: coming from the author of the "End of Controversy," it is deserving of notice.

We know the truth of the story about "the twig" that built the church and school-house. Now that Pat and Jem have got upon the holy wells, we think it would be very desirable if our readers, in various places, would send us the particulars of "holy wells" in their several localities, with a brief account of what is done at them, and whether the practice is declining.

E. C. L.

CHAPTER XXX.

THE SPECIAL PATRONESS OF MEATH.

"Jem, it beats all this time," said Pat, when they next met on the road lately.

"What's in it now, Pat?" said Jem.

"Well, if the Pope is anything at all, he's a greater man than ever I thought he was," said Pat.

"What's his greatness now, Pat?" said Jem.

"Sure, Jem," said Pat, "the Pope has got the Blessed Virgin Mary under his thumb (that's if it's true), and just orders her about, and lays out the work for her wherever he pleases, just as the bishop would with a curate."

"Why, how can that be, Pat," said Jem; "isn't she the Queen of Heaven? and wasn't a new crown put on her in heaven last December, when it was found out, at last, that she was conceived without sin? and, if she is greater now in heaven than she ever was afore, won't the Pope have to take his orders *from her*, instead of going to use her like a young curate just out of Maynooth?"

"Well, Jem, I wonder you are that innocent,"

said Pat ; "sure, wasn't it the Pope that put the new honour on her, and put the new crown on her head ; and if he could do that to her, why wouldn't she have to serve him better, and work for him more nor ever she did ?"

"Well, Pat, there's reason in that, sure enough," said Jem ; "but what has the Pope put on her now ?"

"Well, Jem," said Pat, "sure I got the loan of the *Tablet* newspaper,* and there's the whole story, how the Bishop of Meath had a meeting of a hundred of his clergy, on Saturday, the 21st of July, to tell them the news ; and sure here's the paper for yourself, just to read what he told them."

So Pat pulled the paper out of his pocket, and Jem read—

" His lordship called the attention of the clergy to a communication under date the 11th of February of the present year, which he had had the honour of receiving from the Holy See, and in which the Holy Father was graciously pleased, in compliance with his lordship's humble supplication, to declare the Blessed Virgin Mary *sub titulo immaculatæ conceptionis* (Jem had to

* July 28, 1855, page 472.

spell this part of it) to be henceforth a SPECIAL PATRONESS for the diocese of Meath. His lordship, therefore, instructed the clergy to make known to their flocks the benign condescension of the Holy Father, in conferring this high privilege on the diocese to which they belonged, and also to excite the ardour of their devotion of the Blessed Virgin, *under the illustrious title of the immaculate conception.*"

"Well, what do you think of that, Jem?" said Pat.

So Jem looked back at it again, and considered; and Jem said, "The Bishop of Meath got the start of them, anyway; sure it was about Christmas we heard it was found out that the Blessed Virgin was conceived without sin; and on the 11th of February the job was done, and the Blessed Virgin, conceived without sin, was set down for the diocese of Meath; that was looking sharp, anyway," said Jem.

"Quick work, sure enough," said Pat; "but the bishop was in no hurry to tell the news, when he kept the letter five months in his pocket afore ever he said a word about it."

"How came *he* to be the first?" said Jem, considering.

"Well, he took the notion afore any other bishop," said Pat ; "and mighty sharp it was."

"Wait a minute, Pat," said Jem ; "I wonder is St. Patrick in heaven."

"Well, if he isn't, who is ?" said Pat.

"And why but he asked *first*, when he had the start, and was on the spot ?" said Jem ; "and wouldn't he ask for his own old diocese of Armagh ? I wonder, now, *does* the saints in heaven intercede for the like of them things ? But I'm thinking, now, maybe St. Patrick is at the back of the hills in heaven ; for sure the Protestants say he was a Protestant, and maybe knew nothing about the immaculate conception ; 'cause why, it wasn't found out in his time ; and then how would he get the start about ' *the illustrious title of the immaculate conception ?*' Wouldn't he be ashamed to go to ask the Blessed Virgin any favour about it, and he knowing that he never said one word for it, good or bad, in all his life ? And sure I often think it's little we hear of St. Patrick now, and that little getting less every day ; why, the Catholics seem to think they have got beyond him entirely ; so maybe it wouldn't be any good *his* asking now."

"Why, man alive," said Pat, "don't you see the

job wasn't done in heaven at all, but only at Rome ?"

"Well, that makes it plainer," said Jem. "Sure the bishop would get the start *there* afore St. Patrick. But I wonder *is* the Queen of Heaven under orders at Rome ? Sure that isn't like being the Queen of Heaven at all ! Wouldn't they have to take their orders from her ?"

"Aye ; but if it was the Pope that *made* her the Queen of Heaven !" said Pat.

"Well, that doesn't stand to reason," said Jem ; "sure only God himself could make her the Queen of Heaven. And if He made her queen, would she be under the Pope's orders to run here and there whenever he bid her, to do whatever work he would lay out for her ? Maybe it's to Botany Bay he will be sending her next. But what if it isn't the Pope that's setting her to mind Meath at all ! What if it is herself, and that the Pope only tells what she is going to do herself ! Sure that would be the great thing for the diocese of Meath entirely."

"It would be the fine thing for them that lets lodgings," said Pat ; "sure the lodging money should be higher nor at the salt water itself. Why, wouldn't all Ireland be coming into Meath, the way they would have the Blessed Virgin herself to look after them. But it is my opinion, Jem, that the never a word was said to the Blessed Virgin about it, neither 'by your leave, nor with your leave.'"

"Well, Pat," said Jem, "sure the Pope couldn't have the face to go to put the Blessed Virgin to watch one diocese more nor another, without saying one word to herself about it. Sure, doesn't the Scapular say that the Blessed Virgin appeared to Simon Stock? And isn't there stories about her appearing to the Pope? And who knows but she come to the Pope, or the Pope went and axed her, and she said she was going to mind the diocese of Meath herself."

"Not a bit of it, Jem," said Pat. "Sure, if Popes could talk to the Blessed Virgin that way, wouldn't she have told some of them, afore this, that she was conceived without sin? And more foreby, Jem, it's plain the Pope *didn't* say not one word to her afore he put the diocese of Meath on her."

"And how is that plain, Pat?" said Jem.

"Why isn't it here, in this newspaper," said Pat. "Doesn't the bishop say that it was THE HOLY FATHER that conferred this privilege on the diocese of Meath! And the bishop didn't say, nor the Pope didn't say to him, that the Blessed Virgin said it herself; and if she said one word to them about it herself, sure it's not *that* they would forget to tell?"

"Well but, Pat," said Jem, "sure they might *say* the Blessed Virgin said it herself, whether she did or not."

"True for you, Jem," said Pat, "they might say that, as well as a deal more they do say; but then *they didn't think of saying it.* Sure, if they went to do the job themselves, without ever axing the Blessed Virgin a word about it, or without a notion in their heads to ax her, why then they might *never think of saying* that she said it herself; but if she *had* come to say it herself, *that couldn't be forgot,* and they would be sure enough to tell it. So now you see, Jem, how it is; the bishop and the Pope just got it up between themselves; and they didn't think one bit about the Blessed Virgin that same time, not even enough to see that it would be only decent to tell a lie about her; that's what it is, Jem; and it was the great mistake entirely for them to make."

"But maybe, Pat," said Jem, "when the

Pope has made the Blessed Virgin the special patroness of the diocese of Meath, maybe she just hasn't one hand's turn to do for it more than she had afore; and then, sure, the Pope wouldn't have to go to ask Her at all afore he put it on her; for it wouldn't make any difference to her, and so the Pope might do what he liked."

" And isn't that the pretty humbug to put on the diocese of Meath ?" said Pat; " cocking them up with a fine name as empty as a sucked egg. And if people aren't one bit the better for having the Blessed Virgin for their SPECIAL patroness, how do they know but it's all talk, and no better, about her being a patroness at all ? And sure it's only the Pope's word we have for that, when it's not in the Bible. If the Blessed Virgin is not a bit more of a patroness, and hasn't a hand's turn more to do for her clients, when she is made special patroness, sure it's all humbug the Pope writing over to make her special patroness. And if she *has* more to do for them, when the Pope has put it on her, who's the fool to believe that the Queen of Heaven, if she be the Queen of Heaven, could be ordered about, and more work put on her by the Pope, without so much as a by your leave ? It's making too free with her entirely, so it is, if the Pope believes only the half of what he says about her. It's enough to make us, see the way we are made fools of, in trusting to the Pope's word, and his letters, about patrons."

"But, Pat," said Jem, " tell me this, anyway ; what *will* the people in all the other dioceses say when they see the march that was stole on them, and how the Meath people was up early enough to get the Blessed Virgin, conceived without sin, to themselves, before another could get a chance at her ?"

"Why, then, Jem," said Pat, "if they have any sense, isn't it proud they will be that the Pope didn't go for to make fools of *them*, when he was up to his work."

"Well, Pat," said Jem, " it will be the proud day for Ireland when the people can't be made fools of, with things that no man with sense can believe, in what concerns their souls. But when *will* that day come at all ?"

"When every man has his own Bible in his own hand, Jem," said Pat : "that's the day, and none other."

CHAPTER XXXI,

ARE THE PRIESTS TO GOVERN THE COUNTRY ?

"JEM," said Pat, "I wonder did God Almighty mean that the priests was to govern the country ?"

"Well, Pat," said Jem, "it isn't likely ; for didn't Jesus Christ say his kingdom was not of this world ?* and if the priests are only the ministers of Christ, what business would they have governing the country ? But what set you thinking of that, Pat ?"

"Well, Jem," said Pat, "I got another loan of the *Tablet* newspaper, and it's the greatest paper at all for telling a thumping bit of truth betimes. Maybe a man couldn't make out a newspaper if he hadn't a good bit of truth in his pocket, with a fine bag of lies beside it."

"Well, and what's in the *Tablet* now, Pat ?" said Jem.

So Pat pulled out of his pocket the *Tablet* of August 25th, and they fell to reading the great article in it ; and Pat read out :—

"This country of ours is a Catholic country ; the real constituents of it are the bishops and the

* St. John's Gospel, ch. xviii. v. 36.

priests; we take this for granted, and we do not
see how it can be questioned. There are, of
course, exceptions—places where lay influence
predominates; but, on the whole, the Irish re-
presentation is the work of the priesthood. The
Irish members are in Parliament because *the
priests* have sent them there; they know it
perfectly well, and the Protestants are not
ignorant of it."

"Well, that's true, anyway," said Jem; "sure
it's the priest makes the member, and no mistake.
But why does the people get the worst of it?
What call have the people to it at all? Isn't it
the poor case for them that has votes, to be
ordered one way by the agent and the tother by
the priest? And where's the differ, only that
no one gets beat at a fair or a market for voting
again the agent? But wouldn't it be the fine
thing if Parliament would make a law that the
priests would just send their own members without bothering the people all, and getting them
into trouble? I wonder is that what the *Tablet's*
after? it would be the fine thing for the people
anyway; sure it's the greatest of peace they
would get."

"Well, it would be peace anyway," said Pat;

"but that *isn't* what the *Tablet* set me a-thinking. *Did* God Almighty mean that the priests was to return the members?"

"Well," said Jem, "if the kingdom of Christ isn't of this world, what business would the priests have, only with the kingdom of heaven?"

"Well, it *will* be the great day anyway," said Pat, "when the clergy thinks of nothing only of getting the people to the kingdom of heaven, without harassing them about elections. Maybe it is what Jesus Christ would like, after all."

"Well, now," said Jem, "I'm thinking the clergy ought to keep to the kingdom of heaven. But I wonder how it is in foreign parts, and in America? Is it always the priests that returns the members?"

"Well, man alive," said Pat, "isn't that the very thing the *Tablet* tells us? Sure here it is;" and so Pat read out of the newspaper—

"The *Irish* priests are also the ONLY priests in EUROPE or AMERICA who have such powers. . . . . . They can do in Ireland what the priests CANNOT DO in France, Belgium, or Piedmont."

"Well, if that isn't something to know," said Jem; "and what call have they to it in Ireland,

if they haven't it in any other part of the world ?
Sure it can't be no part of the religion of the
Church of Rome at all ! "

" Well, Jem," said Pat, " it's little I'm caring
now for what's part of the religion of the Church
of Rome. Sure I want to get the religion of
Christ. And did Jesus Christ mean that the
priests was to have the power of returning the
members of Parliament, and governing the
country their own way ? "

" Well, that's clear anyway," said Jem, " that
He didn't mean that at all, when He said his
kingdom wasn't of this world. But if the clergy
could get us good members, what would stop
them doing it ? "

" Well, Jem, you omadhaun," said Pat, " sure
isn't that what the *Tablet* is all about ; just
showing that the members the priests returns is
the greatest set of villians and cheaters in all the
Parliament ! Sure here it is, that the members
the priests send to Parliament thinks of nothing
but asking the Government for 'judgeships,
clerkships, and other favours.' And doesn't the
Tablet 'beg to ask them whether they have not
sacrificed not only the material interests, but
even the spiritual welfare, of the poor Irishman,

to their own political and personal convenience.'
And now, Jem, isn't that enough to show that
the priests is the worst at all to return the
members for the country, when them they sends
thinks of nothing but what they can get out of
it for themselves, and cares nothing at all about
the people ? ''

" Well, sure enough, that's fit for the people to
think about," said Jem.   " But what's 'material
interests,' anyway ? "

" Well, Jem," said Pat, " sure that's the
praties or the meal we eat, and the bit of thatch
on the roof that wants the new straw, or the
rotten sticks that's breaking under it in every
cabin you go into, and the stool that has lost the
leg, and the old pot that's cracked, and the sod
of turf that can't be got, and the window with
the old hat that's stuck in it, and the door that
won't keep out the cowld, and for the ould
blanket and the bed, we'll say nothing of them ;
them's the '*material interests*,' Jem," said Pat.

" Oh, then, sure enough, it's little the priest's
member ever did for the 'material interests,'"
said Jem.   " Sure the Rev. Mr. Owens did more
for that, anyway, when he gave me the blankets
that's over the children.   But what does the

Tablet mean about *the spiritual welfare of the poor Irishman?* What did the priests' members do with that at all?"

"Well, then, Jem," said Pat, "I'm not quite clear about what they done with that; but, sure, here's what the *Tablet* lays the blame on them for;" and so Pat read out of the paper—

"Ireland is not only losing her population, but *the Church* is losing that population in other lands. It is not merely that Irishmen emigrate bodily, but it is that Irishmen *emigrate* SPIRIT-UALLY. This is the question for the con-stituents."

"Them *constituents*, you know, is the priests, Jem," said Pat.

"Oh, then, I know what that means anyway," said Jem, "though I don't see what the members has to do with it; but I know well what *emigrating spiritually* means; sure isn't that what Father Mullin said in his letter,* that the Irish all turns Protestants in America?"

And with that Jem turned round on Pat, and got a grip of his arm, and, says Jem, "Why

* For Father Mullin's letter, in which he calculates that 1,990,000 Roman Catholic emigrants have been lost to the Church since the year 1825, see the CATHOLIC LAYMAN, vol. i., p. 108.

wouldn't we both go to America, Pat, like so many of the boys that wants to turn ? "

" Oh, Jem," said Pat, " don't talk about that ; sure that's what's killing me. Sure I could go to America, and not be ashamed of Christ there, if the wife and childer would beg till I send for them ; but why would I be afraid to confess Christ in IRELAND, and maybe have Him ashamed of me ; and don't talk of what's killing me, now, anyway," said Pat.

So Jem allowed he wouldn't talk about it *then*.

" But if the priests' members is that bad," said Jem, " as the *Tablet* allows they are, does God Almighty mean that the priests is to return the members and to govern the country ? "

" Well, if the priests' members is the worst of all," said Pat, " sure that shows that God Almighty meant the priests to mind the kingdom of heaven, and let the people get the best members they could. But I'll tell you what, Jem," said Pat, " we'll *have* to talk about going to America, or speaking out like men in Ireland."

And if they do we shall have to tell it.

CHAPTER XXXII.

SPEAKING OUT.

"WELL, Jem," said Pat, "it is stuck in me at last; and there's no use talking—I'll have *to do something*."

"Is that in regard of what you were saying the last day, Pat?" said Jem.

"That's it, Jem," said Pat. "I'll have to do what's right."

"And why would you have to do more than you have done these two years back?" said Jem. "Aren't you reading the Bible, and won't that do?"

"Well then, Jem, *it won't;* without we do what is *in* the Bible," said Pat.

"And what's in the Bible?" said Jem.

"Do you mind what we were talking of once," said Pat, "that them that is ashamed of Christ and his words, Christ will be ashamed of them?"*

"Them words isn't easy forgot," said Jem.

"Them words stuck in me all along," said Pat; "and I couldn't quit thinking wasn't I ashamed of Christ and His words, and would not He be

* *Supra,* p. 110.

ashamed of me.   Well, I was reading a while ago in the Douay Bible, and I came on this, ' *If thou confess with thy mouth the Lord Jesus*, and believe in thine heart that God hath raised Him up from the dead, thou shalt be saved. For with the heart we believe unto justice, but *with the mouth* confession is made unto salvation.' "*

"And what would that mean ? " said Jem. " It isn't like confessing to the priest anyway."

" People doesn't go to the priest *to confess Jesus Christ*, but only to confess their sins," said Pat.

" And what does confessing Jesus Christ with the mouth mean ? " said Jem.

" Well, I suppose," said Pat, " when the heathens believed in Jesus Christ, they had to say it out, and go to church like men, instead of pretending they didn't believe on Him."

" Well, that's plain anyway," said Jem; " they wouldn't get salvation by Christ, if they didn't acknowledge Him ; but what has that to do with us ? or how have we to confess Christ with our mouths ? "

" Jem," said Pat, " don't we know that we must believe in Jesus Christ only, and follow His words alone, and nothing else ? "

* Romans x. 9, 10.

"We know that surely," said Jem.

"And if we say that out, that is making confession with the mouth," said Pat.

"It is," said Jem; "there is no use saying against that."

So Pat turned round on Jem, and said, "*Why don't we do it*, Jemmy Brannan? Speak the truth, like a man."

"Why, then, because we're afraid; that's the truth," said Jem.

"We are just afraid of men, and so we are ashamed of Christ and of His words, and we durst not confess Him with our mouths," said Pat.

"Pat, we would be killed entirely if we did it," said Jem; "and get no work neither, and the childer starve or else go to the poorhouse. Wouldn't *that* be the quiet plan for them that turn?"

"Jem, we'll have to come back on the words of Christ," said Pat; "them words won't let us alone." So Pat read out of the Douay Bible: "Fear ye not them that kill the body, and are not able to kill the soul, but rather fear Him that can destroy both soul and body into hell" (Matthew x. 28). "Now, Jem," said Pat, "will something else," said Jem. "Wasn't there a great city then called Babylon ?"

"There was," said Pat ; "for I read about it in the last CATHOLIC LAYMAN."

"It be to be that he was talking about, Pat," said Jem.

"Well, the CATHOLIC LAYMAN allows it was that city he was talking about," said Pat ; "but if he was a prophet, why wouldn't there be another meaning in it too ?"

"And what right would we have to put another meaning on it ?" said Jem.

"Stop a bit," said Pat, "there's more. Didn't the Prophet Jeremiah say that the old city of Babylon would be destroyed ? Sure here it is— 'It shall be no more inhabited for ever, neither shall it be built up from generation to generation' (chap. 50, verse 39). And doesn't the CATHOLIC LAYMAN say that it *was* destroyed 2000 years ago ? and isn't that before Jesus Christ came ? and that it never was built ; and no one ever lived in it since ? Well now, Jem," said Pat, "if the Bible said *anything more* about Babylon AFTER that, doesn't it stand to reason that it *be* to have another meaning ?"

"That stands to reason, Pat," said Jem ; "but

does the Bible say any more of Babylon *after* that ?"

So Pat found out the 18th chapter of the Book of Apocalypse or Revelation. "And now mind, Jem," said Pat; "St. John the Apostle wrote this after Jesus Christ came, and after the city of Babylon was destroyed and never built again; and for all that he speaks of Babylon *going to be destroyed*; for only listen to this :" and Pat read verse 21—"And a mighty angel took up a stone, as it were a great millstone, and cast it into the sea, saying, with such violence as this *shall* Babylon, that great city, be thrown down, and shall be found no more at all." "Now, Jem," said Pat, "wouldn't that be the quare thing to say of a city that was dead and gone long before, if it hadn't another meaning ?"

"It *be* to have," said Jem; "but what more does it say of Babylon ?"

"Here's what St. John says of it," said Pat; and he read out of that same 18th chapter of the Book of Revelations, verses 1, 2, 3—"And after these things I saw another angel come down from Heaven, having great power; and the earth was enlightened with his glory. And he cried out with a strong voice, saying : Babylon the great talking about something *that was to come*, and fitting on the words about Babylon to it. But what was it at all ? Was it the Church of Rome he meant ? That's what we haven't got at yet."

" It's coming, Jem," said Pat ; " it'll be got, that same." So Pat turned to the 1st Epistle of St. Peter, chapter v., verse 13, in the Douay Bible, and he read—" That church that is in BABYLON, elected together with you, saluteth you."

" Sure there wouldn't be a church in a city that was destroyed, and no man living in it," said Jem.

" Well, in course there wouldn't," said Pat ; " but the Douay Bible explains that for us." So Pat turned to the preface printed before the Epistle of St. Peter, in the Douay Bible, and he read—" He wrote it at Rome, which figuratively *he calls* BABYLON." And then said Pat, " If the Douay Bible itself allows that St. Peter himself called Rome BABYLON, why wouldn't we do it too ?"

"Well, that beats all," said Jem ; " Rome is Babylon surely."

" Jem," said Pat, "do you mind all our talk

these two years and more? Isn't it the Church of Rome that sets up other mediators? and tells us to worship Mary and Joseph? and bids us trust in the scapular and blessed medals? and that cuts out God's commandments, for fear we would learn to obey *Him* and not *her*? And, more nor all, isn't it the Church of Rome that says the word of God will set us astray? and doesn't that show *her* gone clean against the word of God? and isn't it the Church of Rome that taught that same to all the world? and what would make her Babylon, if going against God himself wouldn't?"

"Oh, Pat," said Jem, "how *could* we turn at all? sure it's killed we would be entirely."

"Jemmy Brannan," said Pat, "wasn't it you put me on the reading, when I was more loath nor you were, and *will* I go out of Babylon afore you?"

"What *will* we do to get out, Pat?" said Jem; "will we go to America?"

"We *won't*, Jem," said Pat. "Mind you this, Jem," said Pat, "it *isn't* only about getting out: it's about not being ashamed of Christ and of His words; and it's about confessing Him before men, and will I sneak out of old Ireland, only because I'm ashamed of Christ?   And, besides, the children is too many, and will I leave them and Biddy behind me?   And more foreby, Jem, America isn't the place it was : it's getting worse every year on them that goes there, and old Ireland getting better, and the wages good."

"Well, that's what the priests is preaching everywhere," said Jem, "for the people to not go to America, any more."

"Well, I wouldn't blame them, if it was only the good of people they were thinking of," said Pat ; "but sure you know, Jem, the priests have no country, only Rome; and it's Rome they're still thinking of, and not old Ireland ; and it's Rome they're thinking of, and neither Ireland nor America, when they tell the people to stay at home."

"Well, I'm thinking that betimes," said Jem, "but I don't know a'most why."

"I'll tell you why to think of it, Jem," said Pat : "sure I got another loan of the *Tablet*, and here's a letter from Father Reardon* in America to a priest in Ireland, and here's what he says :" so Pat read out of the letter :

"I solemnly believe that if the vessels which

* *Tablet*, Sept. 8, 1855—page 572.

bring them over were suddenly to founder, and carry every creature on board into the depths of the ocean, they would have a better chance of salvation than they have after they have lived for some time in this country."

"Oh, Pat! stop a bit," said Jem, "isn't that the awful thing to think of, of a ship full of creatures, maybe five hundred men, women, and little children, God save us, and the men holding their wives, as I have read in letters, and the poor mothers hugging their little babies on their poor breasts, and all them going down, screeching, at once into the roaring sea to death! and isn't it the cruel thing to hear a priest speaking as if he would *like* that ship to sink! Oh, mercy on us!" said Jem, "sure that's the poor thing."

"Well, sure Father Reardon can have no wife or children of his own," said Pat, "and he mightn't understand our feelings; and why would he stop at that, to save souls in his own fashion? but that isn't the part of his letter I want now," said Pat; so Pat read on.

"So entirely convinced am I of the fearful havoc of souls which is the result of coming here, that were Almighty God to give me the power of building A WALL OF FIRE round Ireland, to prevent its people from leaving it, it should be built before the ink with which I write this line would dry. For the love of Jesus, try to keep your people at home. For every individual you keep, you snatch a soul from hell."

"Well, that's mighty fine," said Jem, "if every one that staid in Ireland would go to Heaven. But it's another thing he was thinking of: them that go to America leaves the Church of Rome, and them that stays in Ireland is afeard to leave it, and that's all one with him as the differ of going to Heaven or Hell: but I am afeard there's a deal of good Catholics in Ireland that won't get to Heaven."

"But what do you say of the wall of fire round Ireland to keep us in ?" said Pat.

"Isn't the fires of Purgatory enough for them to govern us with ?" said Jem.

"'Deed and it's not, then," said Pat, "the people is getting to think little of Purgatory, and that won't keep them in now ; and it's the wall of fire the priests want now."

"And if they had the wall of fire round Ireland, to keep in them that snap their fingers at the priests when they get to America," said Jem, "wouldn't they have a good bit of fire *in the* middle of Ireland too, for the boys that won't mind the priests at home?"

"Well, it's a nice Patrick's Purgatory it would be, more nor even St. Patrick thought of," said Pat, "if Father John and Father Reardon got their way. But it's not come to that yet anyway."

"I'm in dread it's too hot for them that will turn," said Jem.

"Well, Jem," said Pat, "it will be worse yet for them that is ashamed of Christ, and that won't confess him with the mouth. Anyway, that is stuck in me, and I *can't* be without *some* church; and I'll have to find one that will let me confess Christ and his words: that's the church for me, Jem, and maybe I'll find it better here nor in America. My mind's made up anyway, and if I'm beat, sure I can go to America *then* as well as *now;* and not feel then that I'm skulking out of it, like a man that is ashamed of Christ."

So if we should hear anything more of poor Pat's future history, our readers may like to know it, as well as we. For there are clear heads, and some brave hearts too, among the poor people of Ireland; and the humblest of them is worth caring about. Such men may be scarce in Ireland before long: and it concerns us all, that Ireland should not be too hot for them to stay in.

CHAPTER XXXIII.

THE BIRDS.

"Well, Pat," said Jem, when they met again, "are you going to be quiet, or what are you going to do at all ?"

"About what we were speaking of, Jem ?" said Pat.

"Aye, sure that's what we have to think of," said Jem.

"Well," said Pat, "as for thinking, sure I can think of nothing else ; but for *what to do*, sure *that's* the thing to think of."

"Aye," said Jem, "to think how a man will live ; but sure, that's nothing : but to think how will a man give a bit to the childer if he can't get work, sure that's the thing to think of."

"Aye, and the sore thing in earnest," said Pat ; "for a man to take his two choices, to be ashamed of Christ and His Word, or else to have the childer screeching to him for their bit ; and him to see his own children hungry, and give them no more than a stone—that *is* the hard thing, Jem ; and isn't it the hard church that puts a man to that? Is it the church of Jesus Christ at all?"

"Oh, if they would only give us the Word of God; and let us give the childer their bit ourselves," said Jem.

"They can't do it at all," said Pat; "sure they're too far gone for that: sure their church couldn't stand if they did it."

"And what's to be done with the childer?" said Jem. "Sure it's not in man to see them want their bit."

"Is the Bible true at all, Jem?" said Pat.

"Oh, God save us! don't say the like of that," said Jem.

"Is there a word of truth in it at all?" said Pat.

"Oh, sure it's not in earnest you are now, Pat?" said Jem.

"It's in earnest I am now, for the soul that's in me and for the childer that God gave me," said Pat; and then Pat turned round on Jem—"And is it *you* that's in earnest," said he, "about the Word of God? *Is it* His Word at all, or is there any truth in it?"

"It's the Word of the living God, that will stand for ever and ever," said Jem.

" And would you take His word, if He spoke to you?" said Pat.

"Oh, God help me! and isn't that what I would like to do," said Jem; "but isn't it hard when the church stands between Him and me, and between the childer and their bit?"

"Jem, have you sense in you?" said Pat, "and do you think that *it is* the church that stands between us and the hearing of what He says? Sure, *that be* to be something else besides the church that He made Himself."

"It *be* to be something else, that stands between a man feeding his own childer and hearing the Word of God," said Jem; "but what will a man do, Pat, when the childer is crying in the house, and him walking the road and doing nothing? Sure, flesh and blood can't stand it. But what does the Word of God say about it at all?"

"Jem," said Pat, "did you ever see a bird lying dead on the ground, because it was starved?"

"I never did," said Jem; "and isn't that the quare thing to think of, now, in the hard winter, and the long snow we had last spring? and I didn't see one of them dead in the snow; and I didn't think of that before. And how did the creatures live at all, I wonder ! sure there's as many as ever this summer ; and now isn't it a wonder, and we not to think of it ; sure that's another wonder, too."

"I'll tell you why, Jem," said Pat ; "sure here it is in the Word of God ;" and Pat pulled out his Bible, and read it out (Matthew ch. vi., v. 26), "Behold the fowls of the air ; for they sow not, neither do they reap, nor gather into barns ; yet your Heavenly Father feedeth them ; are not ye much better than they ?" "Now, Jem," said Pat, "do you see why you didn't see the birds lying dead in the snow ?"

"Well, it's ever more the little things that's biggest in the Word of God," said Jem. "Sure, the birds gather up nothing for the winter, and still they get through ; sure, it's God done that ; and it's little we think of it, till the Word of God shows it to us."

"Well, sure it isn't for the birds it's written, Jem," said Pat ; "sure it's God that feeds them ; but they can't read it."

"Well, now, I see it," said Jem, "what Jesus Christ said it for ; he wasn't talking to the birds when he said, ' *Your Heavenly Father feedeth them ; are ye not much better than they ?* ' Now, wouldn't that mean that He will care better still for us ?"

"Stop, now, Jem," said Pat ; "there's more." So Pat read verse 33, "But seek ye first the kingdom of God and His righteousness, *and all these things shall be added unto you.*"

"Well, that isn't the way people takes," said Jem. "Sure, everybody thinks they has to look for their bit first ; and if they can serve God after, and make their souls, well and good."

"And isn't that why I axed you if there is any truth at all in the Word of God, or if you will take His Word when He says it ?" said Pat.

"Well, that's new entirely," said Jem ; "but it's not new in the Word of God ; for sure it was always there, only it's new to see it. I wonder how would it be with us now, if we were just to take the Word of God as if He said it to us ? If we were to take Him at His word now, would He do it ?"

"Isn't that just what I axed you, Jem," said Pat. "Would you take the Word of God if He spoke to you, or would you leave it ?"

"Aye, then, I never thought of it that way before," said Jem ; "and it's frightened I was when you asked me would I take the Word of

God; who wouldn't, thinks I; and is the man mad that asks me, or what is he after; is it going to deny it he is ?   And now sure it's the very thing to ask myself, is it the Word of God to ourselves, or is it not ? and will I take it, or will I leave it ? "

" Aye," said Pat, " isn't that what it comes to ? Sure, it's reading the Word of God we are, and don't we *call* it the Word of God ? but *is* it the Word that God says to us, and *will* we take Him at His word ?   If He was to say it to us, would we tell Him we wouldn't take it ? and did Jesus Christ say that for *us*, that if we seek His king- dom FIRST, that food and clothing will be added to us ? "

" And how will it be, Pat, if we just take that same as if Christ said it to ourselves ? " said Jem. " Was it meant, now, just for you and me ? for sure if it was, what would stop me to take the promise of Jesus Christ Himself for the childer and me ?

" Jem," said Pat, " does Jesus Christ tell you to seek the kingdom of God ? "

" What else would I seek in heaven or earth ? " said Jem ; " or what else in heaven or earth would Jesus Christ bid me seek ? "

"Well, then, Jem," said Pat, "isn't it for me and for you, and for every one that has to seek the kingdom of God, that Jesus Christ said this, 'Seek ye *first* the kingdom of God and his righteousness, and *all these things* shall be added unto you?' Didn't He mean just to clear us of them things that stops us, with His own blessed promise, that if *we* seek *that, he'll* mind the rest?"

"And will He do for us and the childer too?" said Jem; "sure that's what goes against us."

We cannot *show* men in our pages : we cannot *show* the power of faith, and the energy in man that springs from a principle Divine. But those who have felt it may imagine the earnestness of Pat, as he exclaimed—

"Will it be worse with us nor with the birds? Will He let *us* die in the snow no more nor them?"

We think that Pat has come near to the kingdom of God. We think he is reading God's Word as if it were in truth the Word of God, that cannot fail to them that lay hold upon it. We think his faith is becoming that victory which overcometh the world (1 John v. 4); the faith of prophets, apostles, and martyrs; the faith of the children of God, that makes them His

children, and lifts up their hearts and hopes to
their Father in heaven. And we shall look to
hear what that faith leads him to do; and what
it brings upon him from that Church which
stands between his little children's bread and the
Word of God.

CHAPTER XXXIV.

OUT OF WORK.

"Well, man, it's long since I saw you," said
Jem, "for I was up the country; and how is it
with you all?"

"Why, then, it's well enough, and it's bad
enough," said Pat.

"And is it done it you did?" said Jem.

"I done it," said Pat, "and I'll stick up to it
now, come what will on me."

"Tell me about it now," said Jem.

"Well, I just went to Mr. Owens' church,
like a man," said Pat; "and I went three Sundays, night and morning, and no harm come on
me at all; and I was thinking, 'maybe it's
not so hard, after all; maybe I'm as safe as the
birds.' Well, it was all going smooth, when
down comes one Dr. Marshall, that was once a

Protestant clergyman in England, to preach in the chapel. 'Well,' says I, 'if a Protestant clergy turns to us, sure I'll hear why he did it;' and to the chapel I goes. Well, who should I see, sitting right fornent the altar, with a big Douay Bible in his hand, but the Rev. Mr. Owens himself. 'Well,' thinks I, 'what will come on it now?' Well, of all the sermons ever you heard, that was the one; it beat ourselves to nothing; and Mr. Owens holding up the Douay Bible fornint him; and sorra one word, good nor bad, Dr. Marshall took out of the Douay Bible, nor no other Bible, from the one end to the other; and, thinks I to myself, if it was the Douay Bible turned you, wouldn't you tell us that, any-way. I'm not going to be worse nor ever I was, thinks I. Well, there was a deal of soldiers there, that was passing through the town, and stopping for Sunday; and when Dr. Marshall began at the Queen in his sermon, the officer just gave them the word, and they all marched out of the chapel, making all the noise you please; and Father Marshall falls to praising the Queen, but not a bit they stopped. Well, that sermon settled me anyway; for sure it's turned his back on the Bible he has, says I; that's the way he's turned. Well, I watched till I seen Mr. Owens going out through the altar rails, and who should up and shake his hand till I thought he would have it off, only Father Corrigan, of Kilbride; for you see he doesn't like a bone in Father John's skin; and so he shook hands with the Rev. Mr. Owens in chapel, afore the congregation; and I mind seeing them two good friends in the relief committee. Well, Mr. Owens comes out, and he goes in the face of all the people to put up a paper on the big tree afore the chapel. Well, he couldn't get it up, and the boys comes round him, and takes the paper, and puts it up for him. Well, and what would it be, only to say he would answer that sermon in church that night. Well, to church I goes; and, sure enough, if the church wasn't full of our own sort, just hundreds of them there. You see he took them so short that the priests could say nothing again it, when the boys was gone out of the chapel. Well, Mr. Owens just answers the sermon out of a face, all out of the Douay Bible; 'that's it,' says I, 'sure that's what I want to hear.' Well, you never seen boys listen better, you could hear a pin drop among them, only one didn't drop, for nobody stirred. Well, when Mr.

Owens was done, the boys all got up and was going without the prayers or the blessing, for they don't get that in chapel, and a decent man stands upon the seat, and, says he, 'Stop, boys, there's more;' and with that they all stopped still, like mice, till the prayers and the blessing was done. Well, thinks I to myself, it's a great sight anyway to see the likes of them here."

"Well, it was a great sight, sure enough," said Jem; "but I'm waiting to hear about yourself, Pat, after what you done; sure that's what I want to hear."

"Amn't I coming to myself as fast as I can, if you won't put me out," said Pat. "Well, Mr. Owens gives out that he would preach to them again that night week. So I goes again, of course; and you know, Jem, there is five roads leading up to the church. Well, who would I pass on the road I went, walking back and forrad, about fifty yards from the church, but Father Peter, that's Father John's curate, looking at every one, and taking their names; and I heard after there was a priest on every road. Well, thinks I to myself, sure I'm done now anyway. Well, I goes on to the church, but there wasn't 10 for 100; for sure they dursn't pass the priest.

Well, it's with Mr. Smith I was working; and, the next day, I sees Father John riding up to the house; it's done now I am entirely, says I. Well, Father John goes to the house, and he goes away again; and Mr. Smith comes into the field, just looking after the work like; and when he comes to me, says he, 'I don't want you after the night.' 'Well, your honour,' says I, 'sure there is not a boy in the field more willing to work.' 'I don't want you,' says he, 'nor the likes of you;' and with that he goes off. Well, I goes home with the sore heart, and not a hand's turn I done from that day to this, and it's the fortnight to-day; and, oh! Jem, it's the sore thing and the cruel thing to walk the roads, just not to hear the childer's crying with the hunger, and to steal into the house after dark, and be kept awake with the poor childer crying. Oh, aren't they the cruel men that won't let the father use his own hands to earn the bit to put into his own innocent children's mouths, and them crying about him with the hunger! Oh, hadn't we enough of that in the famine, and mightn't the priests feel for us now! Oh, is *that* the true sense of the Scripture, at all, at all?" and so Pat began to cry like a child over the children.

"And is there nothing for the childer at all?" said Jem.

"Sorra bit went into their mouths this day; for sure they lived on the one blanket this week, and it's done last night," said Pat.

"Why, then, you'll just bring the cráturs down to me this night," said Jem; "for sure I've the praties, and it's the big pot I'll put on, and they will get their bellyfulls this night anyway; so off with you, man, and bid them stop crying."

So Pat went off in a hurry, and Jem hurried home to get on the big pot.

Well, the children turned to at the praties in style; and when Pat had got his share (for the poor fellow was stinted worse than the rest, to give the children what he could), Pat and Jem fell to talking again.

"And what about the birds, Pat?" said Jem.

"Well, it's thinking of that I am always," said Pat. "It doesn't mean we can't be hungry at all; sure, I know that now; but it means something anyway—it means, anyway, *that God cares for us*; and that He cares for what happens to us; and isn't that something?"

"Well, a man that turns because it's right,

'might starve all out, and his children too,'" said Jem.

"There's no denying that now : he might, if it was the will of God," said Pat.

"Well, there was a deal that never read the Bible, and never thought of God in earnest, that died in the famine ; and, maybe, some that did," said Jem.

"That's true, anyway," said Pat. "I mind the best Christian ever I knew just died for want of the praties, and his children too."

"And what does it mean at all," said Jem, "when Jesus Christ says, 'Seek ye first the kingdom of God, and his righteousness, and all these things shall be added unto you'?" (Mat. vi. 38.)

"There is *one* thing it means, anyway, and *no* mistake," said Pat ; "'Seek ye FIRST the kingdom of God.' Oh, Jem, won't you seek that first ? Sure, there's no mistake in that. Wasn't it you put me on the reading, and will you let me go alone now?"

"Well, that's just what's troubling me," said Jem ; "and there's no mistake in that surely. But what about the rest?"

"Well, then, won't He do what's good?" said

Pat. "He won't keep us alive for ever. And why would we ask it ? isn't it the poor world for the likes of us ? Won't He take us some way ? Won't it be sickness or suffering of some sort ? Sure it be to be *death*; and what signifies the way ? And if He takes us to His glory, sure it won't be breaking His word with us ! And, any-way, the word is good enough to make us trust in Him, while He leaves us here ; and maybe that's the meaning of it. For, sure, He won't keep us here for ever, and why would we ask it ? And when He takes us out of it, sure His own way is the best ; better nor meal, nor praties, nor anything."

"Well, Pat," said Jem, "that's right anyway. Sure, when God pleases to take us, the nothing to eat is no more nor other sickness, when we couldn't eat if we had it. Sure, why does a sick man die, only 'cause he can't eat ? and what does it signify if the praties is there ? But there is one thing hard on me, Pat. Sure, if it was God sent the famine I could lie down and die under His hand, and just put my trust in Him through Jesus Christ ; but when the priest sends the famine on the childer, and him with the whiskey punch afore him quite comfortable, sure that's more nor flesh and blood can stand."

"Well, Jem, I'll put my trust in God, for al the priest can do. And sure there is no saying again' it, He helped me and the children this night anyway, out of your big pot; His blessing on you, Jem, for the good friend you are. And, sure, if I get through till the praty planting, what will I care for Father John and his calling at the altar. Sure, times is turning for us, that way. Sure, Mr. Smith himself would be glad to get me, sooner nor a blackguard at two-and-sixpence that wouldn't do half a day's work of a man like me; but won't I take two shillings afore I go back to *the likes of him ?*"

So Pat and the children went home to do without the blanket; and if we hear of what happens to Pat, we will tell it as usual.

CHAPTER XXXV.

HOW THE PRIESTS GOVERN THE COUNTRY.

"WELL, Pat, how did you get through since?" said Jem.

" Well, I put in the sorest time that ever came on a wife and childer," said Pat. "I stood at the cross, and I offered to work under wages, and not a man would look at me; for Father

John read me out at the chapel, and when work was scarce, and the boys all looking for it, nobody would have any call to me."

"And wouldn't any of the Protestants give you any work itself?" said Jem.

"Well, the Protestants is mighty shy of them that turns," said Pat. "They're afeard of trouble, and they don't like to come under Father John's tongue no more nor ourselves. And besides, the people was riz about the election, and all the blackguards was up, and them paid for mischief, and the railway paid to fetch them on Sundays and week days into Kilcommon from Newtown, the way them that did the beating would not be known, and no one durst go again Father John and his boys while that lasted; and it's myself that got it too, when Father Peter gave the wink on me, and them boys followed me out of the town, and fell to jostling and kicking me."

"And did they hurt you, man?" said Jem.

So Pat put one hand on his chin, and the other to his upper lip, and he pulled his own mouth open, and then he tried to say, "Will you look where my teeth *wor*, Jem?" So Jem looked, and three of Pat's front teeth were gone.

' "Oh, man alive, did the villains do that on you ?" said Jem.

"Why wouldn't they ?" said Pat. "When Father John took the praties off me, why wouldn't they take the teeth ? What call would I have to teeth ?"

"Isn't it the wonder the Government doesn't make a law to let people do as they like and vote as they like, without sticks and stones on them ?" said Jem.

"Well, Jem, isn't there law for that already, only the polis can't be on every road to see fair play. Sure the law is good enough, if the priests would only tell the boys to mind it ; but it's neither law nor gospel with them. Well, I seen one man anyway, and he did it rightly."

"And what was that, Pat ?" said Jem.

"I don't know his name," said Pat, "but he was a snug farmer, and him a Roman, coming in to vote again the priest. And I seen him put his horse in a stable, and his cart on the street ; and he stuck the whip in under the hay, and him just starting down the street to vote. Well, some decent people advised him for to not go down the street, for the boys was killing everyone with the sticks. Well, he just turns and looks down the street, and, sure enough, he seen them at it. Well, the never a word he says, but just takes the whip from under the hay, and the fine new thong it had on it, and away he walks down the street, and him looking that quiet and that bould. Well, I just followed him down a bit, and afore he got fifty yards there was twenty made a run at him with the sticks. Well, he just drew a crack of the cart-whip you would hear a quarter of a mile off, and you never seen a flock of sheep run purtier nor they ran before him. Well, I seen Father Peter come into the middle of them, and says he, 'For shame, boys; is it cowards you are? Go back to him this minute;' and back they went, and the next crack just sent them flying again; and he marched down the street, cracking his whip every foot, and looking at no one, and not one meddled him. Well, that was the time Father Peter gave them the wink on me, and I knowed I was set, and sure enough I was."

"And couldn't you swear it on them," said Jem.

"And how would I know the Newtown boys to swear it on?" said Pat. "Sure, that's the way it's done, by strange boys. And wasn't I told me it was a society in Dublin and in England that allowed every man had rights of conscience to worship God and read his book, and that would help every man to that same when it was took off him. And he allowed it was the Protestant Archbishop of Dublin and the Protestants that done that same. 'I mind that now,' says I. 'Sure I seen a man out of England that told me he went into a meeting, and heard the Archbishop making them a speech, telling them to keep up the rights of conscience; but it's little I thought then it was to send the supper into my poor darlings' mouths, and them at the last shift.'"*

"Well, if that don't come nearer to feeding the birds nor anything ever I heard," said Jem. "If the quality would only mind that advice, and stand up for the rights of conscience for every man to do what he knows is right, that would be the thing to put heart into poor men like us to do what's right. It will be the great day for Ireland when the rights of conscience is free. But how did you come on, Pat, when that meal was out?"

"Well," said Pat, "that got me through till

* We greatly regret that this valuable Society no longer exists.

the weather took up for the praty-planting. So
I takes my spade, and stands at the cross. Well,
who would come by but Father Peter, and says
he, ' Boys, aren't you Catholics, and is it standing with a turncoat heretic you are ?' says he.
' What business has turncoat heretics about the
cross ?' says he. 'Will I be ashamed of you for
boys that won't stand up for your religion ?'
says he. With that I spoke up to him : ' It's the
Queen's street I'm on,' says I, ' and I ax leave of
no man to stand on it. I'm come here to
earn the childer's bread with my own hands, and
nobody else's,' says I. ' You'll have to leave this,'
says he. ' Boys,' says he, ' will you stand it to
have the likes among you ?' Well, with that
Mr. Nulty steps in, hiring men. ' He won't
leave it till I hire him, Father Peter,' says
Nulty. ' Is it hiring turncoat heretics you are ?'
says Father Peter. ' That won't hurt his digging,' says Mr. Nulty. ' Sure, he's the best spade
in the parish, and I'll hire him afore anyone.
Boys, wages is high, and I don't grudge top
price, and over too ; but the man that gives work
for the wages is the man for me,' says Mr. Nulty.
Well, Father Peter got quite mad, and says he,
' If you hire that turncoat you'll not get another

will do more than any law could do towards securing to the people of Ireland the power of being free.   But wages can be raised and obtained at their proper level only by labourers being resolved to give good value for good wages, as Pat intends to do.

We only wish there were more Mr. Nultys in Ireland.

THE END.